HELL SHIP
The Flying Dutchman

The True Catastrophic Events of the Fortuyn as Witnessed by Tom Hardy, the Sole Survivor from the Aforementioned Vessel.

Ben Hammott

Hell Ship – The Flying Dutchman

Ben Hammott

Copyright 2019 ©Ben Hammott

No part of this publication may be reproduced or utilized in any form or by any means, electronic or mechanical, including photocopying, recording or by any other information storage and retrieval system, or transmitted in any form or by any means, without the written permission of the copyright holders.

This is a work of fiction. Names, characters, businesses, places, events, and incidents are either the products of the author's imagination or used in a fictitious manner. Any resemblance to actual persons, living or dead, or actual events is purely coincidental.

Author can be contacted at: benhammott@gmail.com

www.benhammottbooks.com

Book formatted by format-your-book-4u.com

Hell Ship

Author's Note

The writing of this book involved a visit to some Dutch East India Company (VOC - Vereenigde Oost-Indische Compagnie) sites in Amsterdam, as well as research carried out at the Dutch East India shipping archives in the Algemeen Rijksarchief, The Hague, Netherlands. I also visited the full-size replica of a Dutch India vessel, the *Amsterdam*, located at the Amsterdam maritime museum quay.

The existing records of the departure from Texel leading up to the last sighting of the Fortuyn at the Cape of Good Hope provided a starting point for the story of the ship's fateful voyage. I gleaned further details from information and illustrations based on archive records of the Fortuyn and other Dutch ships of the similar period, class and size.

Fortuijn - modernized spelling Fortuin and anglicized as Fortuyn, the spelling used in this book.

The last recorded sighting of the Fortuyn was on 18th January 1773 heading around the Cape of Good Hope when it became parted from the accompanying ships. The Fortuyn was never to be seen again, and its fate is a matter of speculation to this day.

Dutch records show that the Fortuyn was declared missing in 1774, with loss of all crew. Exact date and location are unknown.

The first mention of the Flying Dutchman in print was in 1839 when author Frederick Marryat wrote a novel featuring the ghost ship with a cursed captain named Vanderdecken. Van der Decken can be translated as *of the deck* and thus probably meant "captain of the deck" and not an actual sea captain's name. Sightings of a ghost ship later to become commonly known as the Flying Dutchman began to appear after Wagner composed the opera Der Fliegende Holländer in 1840.

Another origin story points to Captain Bernard Fokke or Falkenberg, who sailed for the Dutch East India Company, as captain of the doomed vessel. He was able to navigate from Amsterdam to Indonesia in just three months, which led many sailors to speculate that he had traded his soul for amazing speed during a game of dice with the devil. That story served as imagery for Samuel Taylor Coleridge's, *The Rime of the Ancient Mariner*, written in 1798.

Almost forgotten nowadays is another phantom Dutch East Indiaman that haunts the Cape; the *Libera Nos*, aboard which Bernard Fokke captains a skeleton crew. No doubt, it is sometimes mistaken for the Flying Dutchman or may even be the real Flying Dutchman. The *Van Diemen*, another Dutch ghost ship, haunts seas closer to modern day Indonesia.

In dramatizing this story, I have taken certain liberties with some of the gathered information.

I hope you enjoy it.

CHAPTER 1

Manuscript

For the tenth time in as many minutes, Vince Parker rearranged the stacks of his latest novel, *Horror Island*, on the table. Sensing the disapproving gaze of the bookshop's owner, Seymore Jessop, whom he had persuaded to let him hold a book signing in his bookstore, he avoided looking in his direction. So far today, only two customers had bought a signed copy, far removed from the fifty to a hundred copies he had told Jessop he would likely sell. That optimistic estimate now seemed as fictional as some of the events in his novels.

While wondering how much longer he should suffer the embarrassing experience, he picked up his signing pen and twirled it in his fingers. His gaze flicked to the entrance when the bell above the door chimed to announce a customer entering. It was an older lady, late fifties, early sixties, Vince thought. Though she didn't seem like someone who would read his books, he wasn't one to assign labels to people on first sight. Her gaze around the store ended on him with a smile. She made a beeline straight to him and held out a hand when she reached his signing table.

"Greetings, Vince Parker. I'm Elizabeth Hardy, a big fan of yours, but you can call me Lizzy."

Vince smiled as he shook her offered hand. "Hello, Lizzy, that makes three today."

The woman glanced around the shop. "It does seem a bit quiet."

"Deathly so," agreed Vince, taking an immediate liking to her. "I heard crickets and glimpsed tumbleweed rolling by a few minutes ago."

Lizzy laughed as she picked up one of his paperbacks. "I've been waiting to read this but held off buying it online when I learned you were holding a book signing here. It's only a short train journey from where I live."

"This signing is something I'm starting to regret, but thanks for making the effort. It's appreciated."

"Good things come to those who wait," said Lizzy with a smile. "Which brings me to another reason why I was eager to meet you, but first, I'd like you to sign my copy." She held out the paperback.

"I'd be happy to." Vince took the book and opened it to the title page. "Would you like it to Elizabeth or Lizzy?"

"Lizzy, please."

Vince wrote a short dedication, signed it and handed it back.

"*For Lizzy, who brightened my day.*" Lizzy read the inscription aloud. She closed the book and smiled at him. "I'm hoping that rings truer than you presently think."

A confused expression appeared on his face from Lizzy's cryptic remark.

"Oh, you can lower those confused bushy eyebrows of yours. I'm not your greatest fan like Annie Wilkes from Stephen King's *Misery*." She pulled a plain cream folder from her handbag and placed it on the table. "Inside is something I believe will intrigue the author in you. I'm heading for a spot of lunch in the Fawcett pub just along the street. Meet me there when you've finished here, and I'll explain everything. They do a lovely steak pie and creamy mash. I'll wait for two hours and then I'm gone." She held out her hand again. "Goodbye, Vince, and I hope you come. It's been a pleasure meeting you."

For the second time, Vince shook her hand. "Likewise, Lizzy."

Without further ado, Lizzy turned away and headed to the counter to pay for the book. Vince returned the wave she gave him when she headed for the exit.

Vince groaned when he spied the owner striding purposefully over.

"Well, Mr. Parker, it's not the rush of fans I was led to believe would descend on my shop to purchase your book, is it?"

Vince shrugged. "It could be worse."

"Worse! I don't see how. You've only sold three copies."

"Less would be worse," offered Vince.

Jessop snorted. "Only barely." He picked up one of the books and stared disapprovingly at the dark, and foreboding cover picturing a spooky-looking island in a storm-tossed sea.

"Would you like me to sign it for you?" Vince asked, feigning innocence.

Jessop promptly returned it to the stack. "How much longer do you intend to prolong your embarrassment? I ask, not to save you discomfort, only because it reflects badly on my shop. Also, you're taking up a lot of room with your tacky display. Space that I could put to better use for books that sell, and make me money."

Vince glanced around at the two sandwich boards with his Horror Island book posters on them. He'd have to haul them back to his car that was parked a couple of streets away. He looked at Jessop sheepishly. "Another hour tops."

Jessop nodded. "Unless we are inundated with your promised hoard of fans and reflected book sales, which seems an impossibility, not a second longer." He turned away and returned to his command post behind the counter.

Vince sighed. His dreams of becoming an A-list author seem to slip farther away to the land of wishful thinking every day. Remembering the folder Lizzy had left him, he opened it and stared at the photocopy of what seemed to be the title page of an old document. The neat, legible handwriting was easy to read: *The true catastrophic events of the Fortuyn as witnessed by Tom Hardy, the sole survivor from the aforementioned vessel.* Underneath in brackets and different handwriting and modern blue point pen was written, *(Fortuyn = The Flying Dutchman).* Though longwinded, it had to be the title of the document absent from the file.

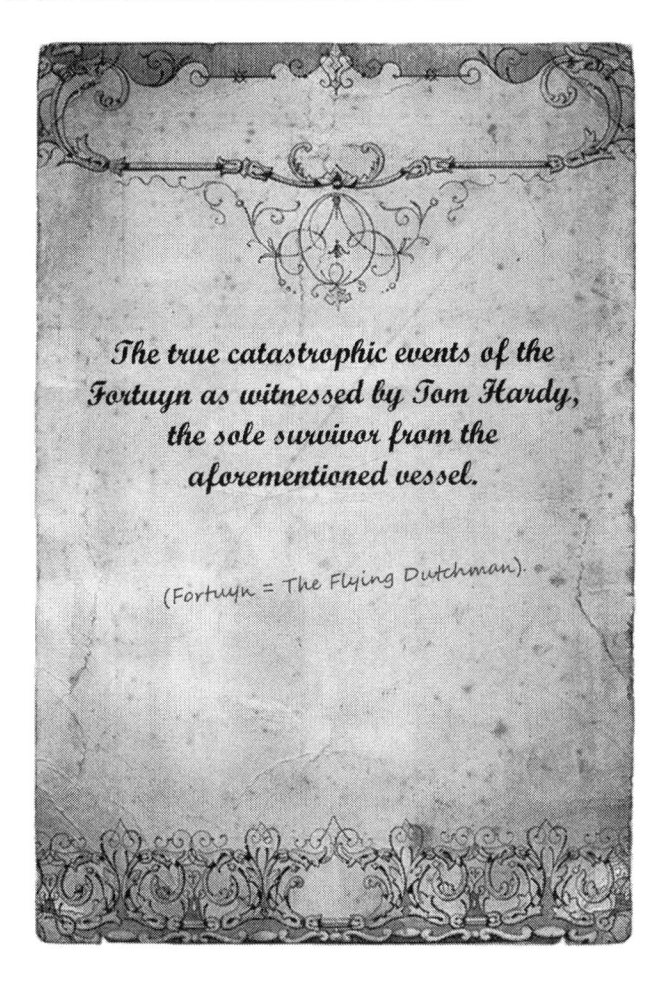

> The true catastrophic events of the Fortuyn as witnessed by Tom Hardy, the sole survivor from the aforementioned vessel.
>
> (Fortuyn = The Flying Dutchman).

He turned the A4 page over; the back was blank. When he reread the title, something dawned on him. Tom Hardy had the same surname as Lizzy. They must be related.

Vince had researched the Flying Dutchman legend for a planned novel he never got around to writing, one of the many he had started but never finished. The ship is nowadays referred to as the Flying Dutchman because some of its early sightings reported the alleged ghost ship as flying above the waves. His research had revealed this spectacle is often experienced, even today when the weather conditions are right and is called a *Fata Morgana*. The optical phenomenon can sometimes create the illusion that a ship on or just over the horizon is floating above the sea.

Lizzy was correct—he was intrigued. He'd stick it out for another hour, clear his stuff and head for the Fawcett pub to meet with her. Hopefully, she'd have the full manuscript with her and let him read it. Why else would she mention it? It could prove to be an ideal subject for his next book.

Vince thought that most people must have heard of the Flying Dutchman legend, though perhaps not as much as the more modern-day Mary Celeste. Everyone enjoyed a mystery, and this was one that had never been solved. It wasn't even known what ship had become the ill-fated ghost ship, but if the title was of a true account, that part was no longer a mystery—it was the Fortuyn. A story about the actual events leading to the demise of its crew could prove to be popular and perhaps the number one best seller he, and most authors, yearned for.

If Tom Hardy had been aboard the Fortuyn and somehow survived, it seems he had recorded what he had witnessed. But why hadn't it been published before now and why hadn't he come forward to let people know he had survived and what indeed happened aboard the Fortuyn? Was Tom the only survivor or were there others who had kept quiet?

His eyes focused on the *True catastrophic events* section of the title. It could only mean something disastrous had happened onboard. His author's imagination went into overdrive as he trawled through different violent scenarios. He glanced at the clock. In about forty minutes, he'd hopefully find out.

◆

Vince placed the photocopied manuscript he had just skimmed through on the table and looked at Lizzie who sat opposite.

"Well, what do think?" asked Lizzy.

"I think it's a fantastic tale."

Sensing Vince's skepticism, she said, "But…"

Vince took a deep breath. "It seems a bit…let's put it this way, and I mean no disrespect, it sounds more like a sailor's ghost story than anything that actually happened."

Lizzie was unperturbed. "Oh, it happened all right." She fished a hand into her handbag, pulled out a slim wooden casket and placed it on the table.

Vince studied the box. It looked old, antique with its Dovetail joints on the corners, and a slight curve to the lid held closed by a simple brass clasp. He tilted it slightly to see the faded image painted on the top. Though faint, it depicted strange creatures climbing the side of a ship. Its crew fired pistols and stabbed at them with swords and flaming torches in an attempt to ward them off. He recognized the scene from the manuscript he had just skimmed through.

"Tom made the box and painted the picture," explained Lizzie. "Once he arrived back in England, he never went to sea again. He recorded the terrible events he had witnessed aboard the Fortuyn to try and stop the recurring nightmares that plagued his sleep. Eventually, they did fade, but he never forgot what happened."

"If the story I've just read is a true account, I'm not surprised," said Vince. Intrigued by the casket, he asked, "What's in the box?"

"Proof," Lizzy replied. "Proof that Tom's story is true."

With eyebrows raised, Vince wondered what the casket could contain that would prove such an unbelievable and fantastical tale was factual. He released the catch, lifted the lid and stared at something wrapped in a piece of sailcloth."

Lizzy pointed at the canvas wrapping. "That is the only surviving part of the Fortuyn that exists. A piece of one of its sails."

Vince fingered the material, an actual relic from the infamous Flying Dutchman, before folding back the edges. With mouth agape in surprise, he stared at what he had uncovered. After a few moments of letting the vision sink in, he raised his head to Lizzy. "Is this real?"

Lizzy, obviously pleased with Vince's reaction, nodded. "It is. Tom brought it back with him. It's the arm the pirate captain Trent chopped off one of the creatures in the story you just read."

Vince returned his attention to the mummified arm chopped off below the elbow. Though only about nine inches long, its sharp claws were frightening. According to Tom's account of events, the creatures had six claw-tipped limbs, making them formidable foes indeed. He scrutinized the arm for any signs of tampering; the finding of strange creatures had been hoaxed before by joining pieces of different species together. Though he was no expert, the claws were like no other he recognized. They had tiny, almost scalpel-sharp teeth running down their cutting edges. They would rip through skin and flesh like the proverbial hot knife through butter.

Now at least believing the monsters in Tom's story might be real, he rewrapped the limb and closed the box. "Okay, I'm ninety percent convinced, but why come to me? You could take Tom's manuscript and the limb to one of the major publishing houses, who would probably jump at the chance and possibly pay you a huge fee for the publishing rights."

"If I wanted money that's exactly what I would have done. As I said when we first met, I'm a big fan of your books. I like your writing style. You get to the point and keep the story moving along without stuffing the pages with wasteful filler. I know when I pick up one of your books I won't want to put it down until I've read the last word."

"Thank you, Lizzy." He tapped the photocopied manuscript. "Tom's account is very factual and will need dramatizing. I'll also have to create some of the events preceding and surrounding Tom's encounter with the creatures, but I promise I'll do Tom's story justice."

Lizzy smiled. "If I thought otherwise, I wouldn't be here."

"Again, thank you, Lizzy. This story could be the big break I need."

"Nothing would please me more. You deserve to be read by a wider audience." She pulled a leather satchel from her bag and handed it to Vince. "Tom's original manuscript."

Vince reverently accepted the package. "Thank you. I'll be sure to return it when I've finished with it."

"No need. Keep it. I'll likely be dead by the time you've finished writing your book."

Stunned by the news, he looked at Lizzy with concern.

"Damn cancer has me," Lizzy explained. "If the chemo doesn't kill it, or me, three to six months, maybe a year if I'm fortunate but unlikely, and I'm gone."

"I'm so sorry," said Vince, who felt genuinely saddened by the news.

Lizzy tutted. "What will be, will be."

Vince nodded a little sadly.

"Tom also invested wisely, so I'm already well provided for." She glanced around the pub that was starting to get busy from the lunch trade. "Now you know why the money doesn't interest me. Even if I needed it, I probably wouldn't be around to spend it, and I'm the last of the Hardy line. The Great Plague killed a lot of the family off when it swept through London in 1666, and we never really recovered. I have something wrong with me below, meaning I never had children to carry on the Hardy line. My husband died a few years back, so I'm looking forward to being reunited with him in the afterlife if such a thing exists. If not, I suppose I'll be none the wiser."

"I'm sorry, Lizzy, but I'm at a loss as to how to respond."

Lizzy reached across the table and laid a hand on his. "A response isn't necessary. Just write the book as fast as you can and then perhaps I'll get to read it before I depart for God knows where."

Vince placed his other hand on top of Lizzy's. "I promise I'll do my utmost."

Lizzy smiled warmly as she retracted her hand and sat back. "I know you will, Vince. You seem like a nice guy, and I hope Tom's story helps boost your career."

"I'm sure it will. There's one thing I'd like to ask, though."

"Please, ask away."

"It's been what, about four hundred years since Tom's adventure? Why didn't he or his family release the story earlier?"

"You have to remember the era when this happened. Back then, sailors were a highly superstitious bunch. Ship owners already found it hard enough to hire crews to risk the long journey to Africa and beyond, and round the infamous Cape that had claimed so many ships and crews. If the story got out there were real-life sea monsters attacking ships in the area; even fewer would be willing to risk the voyage. Even with the evidence of the creature's arm to back up his unlikely tale, Tom was worried, and with good reason I suspect. He believed that if he reported what happened to bring about the demise of all his shipmates, he'd be ridiculed or accused of madness by the wealthy shipowners and merchantmen who would do anything to protect their lucrative trades. That's why he decided to keep quiet and move on. Better everyone outside his family believed all aboard the Fortuyn had perished."

"I feel for Tom," said Vince.

"Oh, from all accounts, he had a good life after the nightmares faded to a manageable level. He married, had kids and lived to a ripe old age." Lizzy glanced at the wall clock and stood. "Time for me to go—hospital appointment." She took a piece of paper ripped from a small notepad from a pocket and handed it to Vince. "My details if you need to contact me."

Vince climbed to his feet. "Thank you Lizzy, you've been so generous. If there's a anything I can do for you, please ask." He took a business card from his pocket and gave it to her. "Now, can I give you a hug?"

Lizzy spread her arms. "Hug away."

They hugged and separated.

Vince picked up the box from the table. "Don't forget this."

Lizzy shook her head. "It's yours now to do with what you will, as is Tom's manuscript. Goodbye, Vince, and good luck with your writing."

"Goodbye, and thanks again, Lizzy. I promise to get the book written before…quickly."

Lizzy laughed. "I'm sure you'll do your best." She gave him a little wave goodbye and walked out onto the street.

Vince sat down, looked at the box and leather satchel containing Tom's manuscript and let out a deep breath. He had a good feeling about this. Thanks to Lizzy, his dream break might have just landed in his lap. Keen to get started on this new venture and contact his agent about this fortunate turn of events, he gathered up everything and headed home.

Travis Atherton, Vince's agent, placed the small casket onto his desk and tapped Tom's photocopied manuscript he had just speed-read. "If this extraordinary tale is real, and I'm not yet convinced it is, you could have a bestseller on your hands."

Vince nodded enthusiastically. "That's what I'm hoping. I've already arranged a meeting with a zoologist, Catherine Dresdale, to see what she can tell me about the creature to which the arm belongs. If I can ascertain it's not of any known creature, then it'll go a long way to shed validity on Tom's story. I've already spoken to someone at the National Maritime Museum in Amsterdam about Tom's ship, the Fortuyn, and it did disappear with all hands in a storm around the Cape of Good Hope. After checking the dates, I found it was only after the date of its disappearance that the sightings of the ghost ship the Flying Dutchman began to occur. I'm heading to Amsterdam next week to go through their archives to see what else I can find to back up Tom's story."

"That's all good, Vince," said Travis glancing at the arm again. "And this Elizabeth Hardy wants nothing for the story?"

"That's what she told me, and she gave me the manuscript and arm. She's a fan of my work and believes I'll do Tom's story justice, which I'll do my utmost to achieve. And as I explained, she has cancer so sadly doesn't expect to be around long enough to enjoy any money she might have been able to get for the manuscript rights."

"That's very gracious of her, but I'd be happier if we had something in writing to legalize your publishing rights. It might prevent any complications further down the line. She may recover and decide she wants some form of payment, especially if it becomes a best seller."

"I truly hope she does recover, and if she does, she has money, so I'm certain she won't change her mind, but I will ask her. However, if she declines, I won't be pushing her into signing anything she doesn't want to."

Travis sighed and shrugged. "Okay, whatever you think is best. I'll get something prepared for you to show her." He scribbled a note on his desk pad to remind him. "When are you meeting with this animal expert? It'll be interesting to find out if the limb's something she's never come across before."

Tom glanced at the clock. "Today, in about an hour at the Natural History Museum, so I had better get a move on." He stood, rewrapped the arm and closed the box.

"Let me know how it goes. Depending on the outcome, I'll start working out the best way to use it and put together a promotional package to present to the publishers when I tout your book around. Hopefully, I'll be able to incite a bidding war."

Vince headed for the door. "Good luck with that. I'll be sure to let you know about any results from the limb. Later then."

Travis raised a hand goodbye, and after Vince had left, pondered which of the big five publishing houses he would contact first if the arm turned out to be from a unique species. Excited by the future deals, he typed *The Flying Dutchman* into his web browser to see how well known it was. He smiled at the almost eleven million results the search term had found. Even if the limb was of a known creature, the book should still achieve reasonable sales, fifteen percent of which would come to him. If there was a movie deal, it could turn out to be a lucrative enterprise for them both.

After arriving at the Natural History Museum, Vince had been led to the back rooms and asked to wait for Catherine Dresdale to come and collect him. She had done so a few minutes later and taken him to her laboratory.

Asking her to play along and he'd explain how it came into his possession after she had examined it, Vince placed the casket on the workbench and watched as Catharine opened it and folded back the canvas wrapping. Her puzzled expression that followed was, he thought, a good sign she didn't immediately recognize the arm.

Intrigued, Catherine slipped on rubber gloves and carefully lifted out the strange limb. After turning it over in her hands to view it from different angles and sniffing it, she looked at Vince. "This is either a clever forgery or from a species I've never encountered before. Where did it come from?"

Vince explained about his meeting with Elizabeth Hardy, and without going into too much detail, a little about her long-dead relation, Tom, and the manuscript he had written from his experiences at sea.

Used to dealing with scientifically-based factual evidence, Catherine raised her eyebrows before refocusing on the arm. "It all seems a bit farfetched to me. However, I must admit the limb has piqued my interest. If you agree, I'd like to take a small sample to test for DNA. If any is present, I'll be able to check it against our extensive database of existing DNA markers for known species. Even if it doesn't result in an exact match, it should reveal to what family of animals it belongs. Essentially, the genetic similarity of organisms is what determines their relation to one another biologically."

"If you don't find a match in your database will that point to this limb being from a new species?"

"Determining a new species is a bit more involved. Usually, except for long-extinct species—dinosaurs, for example—where fragments of fossilized skeletons might be all that is available, a complete specimen is involved. We'll have to wait for the test results, and depending on what they point to, I'll confer with a few of my colleagues to see what we can discover. Even then the difference between species is not meaningful in a clear biological sense. There is no line between *'these are different species'* and *'these are different variants of the same species.'* There's not even a line between that and *'these might as well be brother and sister.'* It's a spectrum."

A bit bewildered by the scientific terminology, Vince asked, "How long until you have a result?"

"Depending on the viability of the sample, with the specialist equipment I have access to here, six to eight hours to get a DNA marker and a few minutes to check it against our database. If the results return a match failure, I'll consult with my colleagues and then contact you with our findings. So, to answer your question, if it's the good news you are hoping for—a new species—it will be tomorrow, but if I find a match, later today." She glanced at her watch. "Make that Tonight."

"That's quicker than I thought. I'm looking forward to learning the results."

"Then I can take a sample?" confirmed Catherine. "I would also like to take some photographs."

Vince nodded. "Yes, please do on both counts."

When Catherine had her sample and photographs, Vince made his way back to the museum's public areas and headed home to start his writing.

Later that night, busy typing at his PC, Vince paused to answer his ringing phone. "Hi, Vince speaking."

"Hello, Vince, it's Catherine from the Natural History Museum."

Expecting bad news because she had rung tonight, Vince's face dropped. "Hello, Catherine, how did the results go?"

"In your favor. I was going to wait until tomorrow, but I thought you'd like to know my preliminary thoughts."

Vince perked up. "Thank you; I would."

"You'll be pleased to learn that I failed to find an exact match for the DNA sample I took with any on our database. Its closest neighbor seems to be cephalopods. To elaborate; the taxonomy of life on Earth is divided into five or six *kingdoms,* one of which is *Animalia,* the animals. One *phylum* within Animalia is *Mollusca,* mollusks, and one *class* within Mollusca is *Cephalopoda,* cephalopods. The modern cephalopods are octopus, squid, cuttlefish, and nautilus. A fun fact is that nautiluses can have up to ninety arms, shells and have been around for five hundred million years. There are many extinct cephalopods, including a large subclass of ammonites that we know from their abundant fossil remains. But what is strange and has some of us a little excited here is that there also seems to be a remote link with species in the arthropod phylum. These include the group of invertebrate animals with jointed legs and an exoskeleton. Their relatives include scorpions, crabs, mites, insects, crustaceans, lobsters, prawns, and centipedes and millipedes. Spiders and octopuses are in the phylum Mollusca, but the arthropods and the mollusks branched off from the same ancestor at least seven hundred million years ago, so to find one significantly bearing all these traits still alive a few hundred years ago—and probably still alive today—is extremely exciting."

"Wow! It's a lot to take in, and I don't pretend to understand all of what you've just told me…"

"Sorry, it was a bit of an info dump, but that was my layman's explanation. I'll try and make my report easier for you to understand."

"Appreciated," said Vince. "However, what I think I gleaned from your information is that the creature the limb came from is a new species as far as you can determine and that you think it might be from a species that has been around for millions of years."

"Basically, yes, and there are precedents," replied Catherine. "With none or just little changes to their prehistoric appearance and behavior, creatures roaming the earth, seas, and skies millions of years ago can be found in the modern world from scary descendants of prehistoric deep-sea sharks to a 120 million-year-old ant. A few examples are imperial scorpions that have been around for four hundred million years; tadpole shrimp for three hundred million; and jellyfish for six to seven hundred million. The horseshoe crab, considered to be the closest relative to the legendary trilobite, ranks among the most well-known of the living fossils, having remained virtually unchanged for an astonishing four hundred and fifty million years. Lastly, there is the coelacanth, which has physically evolved over the last three hundred and sixty million years, and until it was discovered still living in nineteen thirty-eight, was thought to have died out sixty-five million years ago during the great extinction in which the dinosaurs disappeared."

"Although I've heard about the discovery of the coelacanth, I didn't realize there were so many more creatures still around from the dinosaur age."

Catherine laughed. "The dinosaurs occupied a relatively short period in the scheme of evolution, having first appeared in the Triassic Period around two hundred and forty-five million years ago. The species your creature is from would have witnessed them come and go. Though I'm certain there's no connection, one species, Lampreys, reminds me of the behavior of the tentacles on the larger creature and the kelp stalks you mentioned. Lampreys are jawless fish characterized by a many-toothed, funnel-like, sucking mouth that thirty-eight of their known species use for boring into the flesh of other fish to suck their blood. The oldest lamprey fossil found in South Africa dates back to some three hundred and sixty million years ago, but its striking resemblance with modern specimens is indisputable."

"That's amazing," exclaimed Vince, wondering how much of this information to include in his book.

"It sure is. I've set up a meeting with a few of my scientific colleagues tomorrow morning to discuss my findings. I'll contact you with the outcome before I write up my report, but I'm confident you can expect more favorable news."

"Exciting," said Vince. "And thank you, Catherine."

"My pleasure, Vince. If, as I suspect, we determine this is a new species with a lineage millions of years old, then I would, with your permission, like to write a paper on it for a scientific journal."

"Please, feel free to do so. It's the least I can do to return the favor."

"Thank you. Well, until tomorrow."

Vince said goodbye and ended the call. This exciting news could only bode well for his book. Excited by the prospect, he rang his agent to inform him of the fortunate turn of events. Tomorrow he would contact Lizzy to let her know the limb's DNA results backed up Tom's story.

CHAPTER 2

Finished

It took Vince three to research and write his dramatized account of Tom's story, which had included a visit to the National Maritime Museum in Amsterdam to browse through their extensive archives on the Dutch India Company and ships of the era. It had proved to be a fruitful and worthwhile trip. To get the feel and layout of the type of vessel that Tom would have been aboard, he also visited the impressive full-size replica of the three-masted "*Amsterdam*" located at the Amsterdam maritime museum quay. The Amsterdam was a large vessel of the Dutch East India Company, which on its maiden journey to Batavia in the winter of 1749 sank in a storm in the English Channel. Its remains were found a few years back, prompting the building of the replica.

Vince had just completed the final edit the day before, and after a final readthrough, he would hand it over to Travis. After converting it into a Mobi file, he transferred it to his Kindle reader, stretched out on the sofa with a pad and pen beside him to jot down any required edits, and started reading.

TOM'S STORY

The True Catastrophic Events of the Fortuyn as Witnessed by Tom Hardy, the Sole Survivor from the Aforementioned Vessel.

My name is Tom Hardy and I have a tale to tell many will not believe. That, however, is not the reason for me writing my story down. It is an attempt to banish the awful nightmares that plague my sleep. I am putting quill to paper to recount the reasons for them. Hopefully, turning these images into words will transfer them from my thoughts onto paper, which I can then lock away until one day when I am long dead, the truth about what happened will finally be revealed.

The events leading up to my ill-fated voyage and my resulting nightmares begins innocently enough, and if I had known then what I know now, I would not have set out on my fateful journey.

It begins in April in the year of our Lord, 1793.

With my yearning for adventure and to see more of the world, I had little interest in working at my parents' apple orchard in Somerset. I wanted to go to sea and travel to exotic lands. I could read and write, so other options were open to me other than apple picking, but I chose adventure. Though my parents were at first against it, they realized tending the trees and picking apples to be turned into cider held no excitement for me, and eventually relented. Hoping I would get it out of my system and would then settle down into the family business, at the age of seventeen they bid me farewell and safe travels.

Brimming over with excited anticipation at the adventures I would surely have, I traveled to London and headed straight for the main docks to seek employment. It was a noisy, bustling place. Cargo from countries I had never heard of was unloaded into barges heading to other destinations along the bustling Thames. At night (and sometimes during the day) the River Pirates, Night Plunderers, Scuffle-Hunters and Mud Larks, attacked vessels or broke into warehouses to steal the lucrative cargo. Spices were a particular favorite of these nefarious vagabonds; light to transport and easy to sell.

After spending a couple of months of part-time work helping to load the barges, I met Wagner Mesling, a Dutch sailor who spoke surprisingly good English. He worked for the Dutch East Indian company. We became friends, and when I told him I was looking for adventure, he knew just the place where I could find it; aboard one of the East India vessels. He secured me a position as the assistant cook on the ship he was taking back to Holland.

Six weeks later, Wagner procured a further position for me on the same ship he had found employment on as a seaman, and I was to be the cabin boy aboard the Dutch East India vessel, The Fortuyn.

It was with a sense of high adventure and excitement that I set sail on my first voyage to a strange land. I was heading for Java.

My first voyage was also to be my last. By the time I returned to England a little over a year later, I would be a changed man with the thirst for adventure and excitement completely expelled from my being.

A warning to all who may come across this document in the future; what you are about to read is not for the fainthearted. If you are of this disposition and don't wish to be plagued by similar nightmares as I have endured, then I implore you to stop, look away, and read no more.

What follows is my harrowing voyage aboard the Fortuyn and beyond.

CHAPTER 3

No Headway

The storm, formidable and ferocious, had appeared out of nowhere, as is often the case around the Cape of Good Hope, commonly referred to as the Cape of Storms. It tossed about the Dutch India ship, the Fortuyn as if it were a child's toy. Brutal and savage, the gale-ravaged waves smashed against the hull as if determined to destroy the obstruction in its path, something its crew thought likely based on the disquieting creak of hull timbers. Spray continually washed over the deck from all sides and drenched the anxious sailors battling the storm. It had arrived so suddenly they'd had no time to reset the sails, a task they were now trying to undertake while it raged.

Tossed about by the erratic pitch and roll of the ship, the crew climbed the rigging whipped back and forth by strong gusts. Those working on rain-slick wooden yardarms with heavy, water-soaked canvases carried out their toil while trying to prevent themselves from being thrown off to be dashed to the deck far below or ditched into the cruel sea. Both would prove equally fatal. The air was thick with the angry sea's pungent, salty stench that worked its way into every crevice above and below decks.

The Dutch captain of the stricken vessel, Bernard Fokke, steadied his stance against the swaying quarterdeck and peered through his telescope at the distant ship far beyond the bow. The *Maira*, his companion vessel for the voyage from Batavia to Amsterdam, was also a ship of the Dutch East India Company. Though both ships were of a similar design and size, and on the same tack, strangely the Maira had made better headway and was drawing quickly from their sight. The Fortuyn seemed unusually sluggish as if Neptune or the Devil held them back.

Fokke glanced up at the flapping sails and thrumming lines where men high on the stern mast's yardarms furled the sails to prevent the ship from slewing in the gusts, which could prove disastrous in a storm this powerful. He switched his focus to the men on the foremast, occupied with double-reefing the mainsail and foretopsail, and then looked at the billowing jib as he pondered the notion of bringing more forward sail into play in the hope they'd make better headway against the storm. If they could round the Cape, they'd be out of the worst of it and might be able to reach the safety of the port at Cape Town. His gaze flicked to the stormy sky when the dark clouds flashed with internal lightning, illuminating their swirling masses. They gathered together, blocking any remaining daylight, blanketing the erratically tossed and rolling ship in the gloom as thick as the crew's somber mood. As thunder rolled through the heavens, rain fell, adding to the crew's misery.

"Light the lanterns," shouted the boatswain from the mid-deck, his booming voice loud enough to be heard against the wind screaming across the ship like phantom banshees rejoicing in the ship's distress and willing all aboard to their doom.

Fokke gazed the length of his struggling vessel. He could scarcely see the forecastle in the darkness shrouding his ship. Patches of orange light, barely adequate to chase away the shadows, appeared along the decks as the crew lit the lanterns.

The first mate, Collas Drasbart, gripped the rail when a powerful swell lifted the ship before slamming it back into the sea with a violent jolt. Men knocked from their feet slid across the sloping deck and grabbed at the rail to stop themselves from being flung into the swirling ocean. A man overboard in this weather wouldn't survive for long.

"Perhaps we should consider turning about to seek a safe harbor until the storm blows itself out, Captain?" suggested Drasbart.

Fokke turned his head to his first mate. The captain was renowned for the speed of his trips to and from the lucrative Netherlands to Java trade route, causing some to suspect him of being in league with the Devil. His secret was that he took a different course to most, one that took advantage of favorable winds and currents, shaving weeks off the trip. "We press on," stated Fokke firmly. "We've ridden through worse and survived, so I don't expect us to falter this time."

"Aye, sir." Drasbart frowned at the huge rolling swells. Luckily, they had a full hold to give the ship some stability against the raging weather.

Fokke turned his head to the helmsman when the bow turned slightly and noticed him straining on the wheel. "Hannigan!" he shouted to be heard. "Straighten her up, man, before we turn side on to the storm."

Hannigan was grunting in his efforts to turn the wheel, well aware that if the vessel turned broadside to the weather, the hull would likely breach. A capsizing was what all sailors feared, especially in a storm as ferocious and unforgiving as the one they were currently battling. "There's something wrong, Captain," he yelled back. "She's fighting me."

Shoving his spyglass into his first mate's hand, Fokke crossed to the wheel and grabbed it. Struggling and with much effort, between them, they slowly turned the ship's bow into the storm again.

The boatswain, Jozef Janzen, had felt the ship turn, and sensing something was amiss, he climbed the steps to the quarterdeck. Spying the helmsman and captain fighting the wheel, he grabbed a securing rope, slipped the noose over a handle and pulled it tight to take up the slack.

Letting go of the wheel, Fokke nodded his thanks to his boatswain. "She's pulling to starboard for some reason."

"Aye, I noticed, sir," said Jozef, worry creased his sea-worn features. "Storm-damaged the rudder, you think?"

"Ain't that," stated Hannigan confidently. "Something's pulling her."

Hannigan was an experienced helmsman and one of the best he had sailed with, so Fokke trusted his judgment. "Could the current be responsible?"

Hannigan shook his head. "Unlikely. Feels more like a fouled rudder."

"If that's the case there's nothing we can do to remedy it until the storm's released us," said Jozef.

Staring at the creaking rope straining from its efforts to prevent the wheel from turning, Fokke cursed his luck. "Let's double-lash the wheel in case she goes the other way and get two men up here to assist Hannigan keeping us headways until the storm's passed."

"Aye, Captain," acknowledged the boatswain, moving swiftly to double-lash the wheel before climbing down to the mid-deck to choose two men to aid the helmsmen.

Fokke crossed to his first mate and took back his spyglass, now useless in this light. "I'll be in my cabin if I'm needed."

"Aye, sir." As the captain left, Drasbart walked to the front of the quarterdeck and peered down at men rigging safety lines and adding an extra rope around one of the large water barrels that showed signs of breaking free. He directed his gaze upon the cabin boy who suddenly appeared from below deck, rushed to the rail and spewed his dinner over the side. A flash of lightning lit up his sickly pallor. It was the boy's first voyage. At seventeen years old, he was the youngest soul aboard. Drasbart descended the steps.

Tom Hardy retched until his guts were empty. When lightning flashed its stark light on the angry waves, he noticed something around the hull.

"Don't worry, son; the sickness will pass."

Tom wiped his mouth with the back of his hand as he turned to the first mate. "Sorry, sir."

"No apology required, young Tom. This storm is rough enough to send the hardiest sailors to the rail."

"I think I saw something in the sea alongside the ship."

"Yer did?" Drasbart moved to the rail, and gripping it with his hands to prevent being launched over the side by the lurching ship; he peered down. If there was anything below, the darkness concealed it.

"I think it was kelp, sir," answered Tom, fighting down the bile his churning stomach hurled up his throat.

Drasbart gazed around the heaving deck. Spying the boatswain, he called out, "Jozef, a lantern."

Jozef was at his side in moments with the requested lantern."

"Hold it over the side. Tom said he saw weed along the hull."

As instructed, Jozef joined Drasbart and Tom peering down at the mass of seaweed highlighted in the lantern's orange glow. The thick leaves were about a foot wide and three times that long. Some of the broader, rounder leaves had stalks with strange, elongated flowers sprouting from them; their petals closed as if protecting themselves from the raging tempest.

"Storm must have dragged it free from the seabed," offered Jozef.

Drasbart took the lantern and shone it along the side of the ship. The weed stretched out for a few yards from the hull, then continued sternward. On some of the leaves, attached by a finger-thick stalk, were pale objects the size of a slightly stretched ostrich egg. Translucent in the lantern light, there was something dark within. Tendrils sprouting from the stalks held the leaves together in a leafy net and had what looked like suckers on their tips that swayed serpent-like in the air. Whether the swaying was by purpose or put into motion by the storm was difficult to determine.

Jozef swept his eyes over the sucker tendrils nearest the hull to find they were attached to the ship. "The damn stuff's holding on to us," he exclaimed. "It must think we're the seabed or a rock or something."

With a creased brow, Drasbart looked at the boatswain. "You ever seen kelp like this before?"

Jozef shook his head. "The sea be full of strangeness and she ain't none too quick to give up her secrets."

"What's that over there?" called out the sharp-eyed cabin boy when another lightning flash lit up the ocean.

Drasbart directed the light where Tom pointed, and all three stared at the dolphin snared by the seaweed. Its lack of struggles indicated it was no longer alive. Sucker-tipped tendrils attached to the dolphin throbbed as if they were pumping something through them.

"It seems to be feeding on the dolphin," said Jozef, shocked by the revelation.

"Plants don't eat animals, do they?" asked Tom, fascinated, his nausea temporarily forgotten.

Drasbart shrugged. "It seems this type does."

When he held the lantern higher, the light revealed five more dolphins being feasted on by the flesh-eating plant. Some were little more than bones stripped of flesh.

Jozef pointed at one of the roundish, egglike objects. "What do yer think those things are?"

Drasbart shrugged. "Seed pods, I suppose."

Jozef ran his eyes over the blanket of weed. "At least this explains what's been slowing the ship down and likely fouled the rudder."

"We'd better let the captain know." Drasbart turned to the cabin boy. "Tom, go inform the captain of what we've found here."

"Aye, sir." Using one of the safety lines to steady his footing on the pitching deck, Tom headed for the captain's cabin.

Drasbart turned to Jozef. "Let's check around the hull to see the extent of the weed that has us in its grasp."
Jozef grabbed another lantern, and together they walked along the rail intermittently shining the light over the side.

◇

The captain sat at his desk writing up the storm in the ship's log. Hampered by the lurching, wave-ravaged vessel that caused the lanterns to swing, constantly throwing moving shadows across his work, he finally gave up, closed the book and stowed it in a desk drawer.

Fokke turned to the door when someone rapped softly upon it. "Enter."

"What is it, Tom?" inquired the captain, when the cabin boy entered.

"Mr. Drasbart sent me to inform yer there's seaweed around the ship, Captain. Some peculiar kelp weed that eats dolphins."

Fokke's eyebrows rose disbelievingly at the inconceivable report as he scrutinized the lad. "Dolphin-eating kelp is it, me lad?"

The boy nodded. "It also has hold of the ship. Boatswain thinks it's what's slowing the ship and fouled the rudder."

Finding it hard to believe but seeing no sign of deceit in the lad's face, Fokke rose from his seat and crossed to the bay window almost stretching the width of his cabin. Wind and sea spray blasted him when he opened a window and poked his head out. His gaze down at the mass slightly darker than the sea proved the truth of the boy's report. Pulling his head in, he unhooked a lantern and returned to the window. The lamplight picked out the tendrils attaching the strange kelp to the hull and stretched out behind the ship like a bride's train. Some leaves and tendrils had climbed so far up the stern they were close enough to touch. He focused his gaze and the light on the nearest of the bizarre pods dotted across the kelp and wondered at the nature of the dark thing within. If it was edible, it might be a welcome source of fresh food — payback for the kelp inconveniencing them the way it had.

Fokke pulled his head inside and held his hand out to the boy. "You got your knife with you, Tom?"

Nodding, Tom pulled his knife from its sheath on his waist as he crossed the room and placed it in the captain's hand.

Fokke handed Tom the lantern. "Hold it by the glass, so the light shines through."

Tom did as he was ordered and pressing his nose against the cold glass, watched the captain stretch down and cut free one of the pods.

After bringing it inside, he crossed to the map table that sat in the middle of the room and doubled as a dining table when required. He placed the pod on it.

Tom fastened the window, crossed to the table and observed the captain cutting along one edge of the pod. Both he and the captain gasped when something flopped out with a squelch, filling the room with a stagnant stench.

Both stared at the small pale creature covered in a milky gelatin substance and tiny scales. On its back were what seemed to be short, thick hairs. After a few seconds of stillness, it jerked and began to squirm weakly. What appeared to be a sucker stem acting as an umbilical cord attached to its belly slipped out of the severed stalk and oozed a thick yellow liquid that pooled on the table. As if smelling the foul goo, the creature unfurled its two front limbs, dug talons that tipped each one into the table and dragged itself around to it. A long, thin tongue slithered from its pointed mouth and lapped up the yellow sludge. When that was gone, it started eating its umbilical cord.

"I've never seen the like," stated Fokke, staring intensely at the strange sea creature ripping into its self-cannibalistic meal.

"It's a strange beast, true enough," observed Tom, a little scared of the vicious creature. "Will yer throw it back into the sea?"

Fokke dragged his gaze away from the feasting creature and looked at the boy. Ever conscious of making a profit, he had a better idea. The strange new species might be worth something to someone. "No, go find something to catch it in. Something we can seal."

Though uncertain it was a good idea, Tom wasn't about to argue and went to find a suitable container.

The captain's voice halted Tom's rush out the door. "You should find something in the hold. If not, ask the cook."

Tom nodded and closed the door behind him.

Fokke poked at the creature with the knife and gasped, snatching his hand away when it reacted with such speed, its movements were impossible to follow. It leaped at its attacker, wrapped its limbs around the knife and clamped its teeth on as best it could. What he thought were hairs on its back proved to be thin tendrils that grew and stabbed at the knife, as if trying to penetrate it. When they failed to do so, the tendrils retracted. The creature released its hold on the thing that could not be killed or eaten and returned to devouring its cord.

"Will this do?" asked Tom, entering.

Taken aback by the creature's viciousness and speed against an attacker, Fokke glanced at the small, wooden rum barrel Tom held and nodded.

Tom plucked his knife from the table, prized off the lid and looked at the creature. "How do yer want ter do this, sir? Will yer pick it up and drop it in?"

After what he had just seen, Fokke wasn't certain he wanted to do it at all. He certainly wasn't going to put his hands anywhere near the vicious thing. "We'll put the barrel over it and then slide the lid underneath to trap it inside." He took the cask from Tom. "We'll have to be quick, though. It's a fast bugger."

"I assure yer, Captain, there won't be no dilly-dallying on my part."

"Okay, get ready?"

Concentrating on the creature that had returned to its feast, Tom held the lid ready.

Fokke stretched the open end of the barrel towards the creature and then suddenly lunged at it. He slammed it down on top of the creature. It screeched, angrily it seemed, at its imprisonment and scratched frantically at the cask.

"Quick, slide the lid under while I release the pressure slightly," ordered Fokke.

Worried the enraged beast would attack if it got free, Tom placed the lid on the table beside the barrel and slipped it underneath. He felt the creature attacking it as he slid it in until only a slither of it remained visible. "That's as far as I can get it. Yer needs ter come my way a touch."

Fokke glanced at the askew lid and shifted the barrel until it dropped in place. Due to the recess in the cask top, they wouldn't be able to secure it firmly until it was turned over.

"Stand back, Tom. I'm going to get a hand underneath and flip it over."

Hell Ship

Tom backed towards the door, prepared to rush out if the creature escaped and came anywhere near him.

Fokke took a deep breath, slid the barrel to the edge of the table, so it overhung slightly and pressed his fingers against the lid. Inch by inch he slid the cask off the table until he had his whole hand pressed against the top. In a quick movement, he flipped it over and put it on the table. Keeping it secure, he thumped the lid with the edge of his fist until it was seated firmly in place. As the creature scratched frantically at the walls of its prison, Fokke slowly released his hand and let out the breath he hadn't realized he was holding. He smiled at his accomplice.

"We did it, Tom."

Tom stared at the barrel, wobbling with the trapped creature's frantic attempt to escape its prison. "Will it be able to breathe in there?"

"Good point." Fokke turned the cask and unscrewed the dispensing tap. The small hole should let enough air in and provide a means to feed it. "Now go fetch the carpenter and bring him back here with a hammer and some small nails to secure the cask lid so it can't escape. Once he's finished, put it in that chest," he pointed to a large sea chest against one wall, "and then come and find me to let me know you've completed the task."

"Aye, Captain." Tom headed for the door.

"And, Tom, you did good," praised Fokke.

Tom smiled and left to fetch the carpenter.

Wondering what part of Hell the sea had dragged this strange creature from, Fokke stared at the small claw it poked through the hole and prodded around the edge as if testing the strength of its prison. Surely such a unique species would be worth something to someone. A zoo, museum, or one of those traveling shows that display the unusual—and at times, horrific—oddities of human and animal deformities. Using a rag to mop up the foul substances from the egg from off of the table, he bundled the mess up and threw it out the window. Grabbing his coat, he headed topside to find out the full extent of the weed problem.

Drasbart and Jozef had walked a complete circumference of the ship to determine the scope of the kelp problem, and it wasn't good news.

"If there was any doubt before, there isn't now," stated Jozef. "The weed *is* slowing us down, but what's more of a concern is that it's fouled the rudder. If the storm carries us towards the Cape and the rocks, we might not be able to turn away.

Stepping into the brunt of the storm, Fokke heaved the aftcastle door shut. With windborne spray and rain pricking his face, he gripped one of the safety lines to keep his balance and searched for his first mate. Spying him at the port rail with the boatswain, he fought the wind and roll of the ship as he crossed the deck.

"How bad is it?"

Drasbart turned to see the captain beside him, peering over the rail at the kelp highlighted in the boatswain's lantern light. "Stretches from mid-ship to stern and seems to be creeping nearer the bow."

"We'll have to cut it free, or we'll never make any headway," stated the captain.

"Will be difficult in this weather," replied Drasbart.

"Nevertheless," said Fokke. "See that's it done and quickly."

The first mate nodded. "Aye, Captain," and watched Fokke head for the quarterdeck.

"We might be able to free it with the boathooks," suggested Jozef.

Drasbart nodded. "Do it. Collect as many as you can and share them amongst the men. Divide them into pairs so one can steady the man with the boat hook to stop him falling overboard."

Jozef moved off to carry out his task while the first mate returned to the quarterdeck and explained the plan to the captain.

"If all goes well, that will see the end to the problem, and we can start making some headway against the storm."

"Hopefully that'll be the case," said Drasbart. "It does explain our inability to keep up with the Maira."

"We'll still beat her back home to Amsterdam," stated Fokke confidently with a knowing smirk.

CHAPTER 4

Retaliation

Guillermo steadied himself against the weight of Pepijn, who was attached to the rope tied around his waist. Ducking to avoid the end of the boathook that narrowly missed striking his head when Pepijn swung it over the side, Guillermo rolled his eyes at the boatswain beside him.

"The man's a menace with that thing."

Jozef smiled as he leaned over the rail to observe Pepijn, his hands gripping the side against the rolling ship.

In the light shed by the lantern hanging from the rail, Pepijn picked out his first target; the nearest plant suckered to the hull, and he stretched out the boathook. He slipped the curved piece of metal under the stalk and pulled, but it stubbornly refused to release its grip. Not to be outwitted, Pepijn yanked the hook hard. It became detached and flopped about wildly as if surprised by its abrupt freedom.

Pepijn's success was short-lived when the sucker reattached itself to the ship. Cursing the seaweed, he tried again. The freed stalk again flopped about for a moment before it lunged at the hull and secured itself again. Straightening up, Pepijn turned to the boatswain.

"It's not working. Every time I pull it free, the damn thing re-attaches itself."

Jozef nodded. "I saw."

Guillermo considered the problem for a few moments and pulled out his knife. "If we tie the knife to the end of the pole, we could try cutting it free."

Pepijn grinned. "Slice through the bugger. I like it."

Jozef thought it was a good idea. "If the sucker's not attached, it won't be able to grip on again. Do it."

After a few minutes toil, they had the knife attached to the handle end of the boathook. Pepijn leaned over and slashed at the obstinate vine. The blade sliced through the stalk without resistance. The severed stem sprayed dark ooze as it swayed wildly as if silently screaming.

Pepijn turned to Guillermo and the boatswain. "It worked."

"Carry on cutting free as many as you can reach, and I'll inform the others of the new technique."

As Jozef walked away, Pepijn selected another stalk and sliced through it. He then moved to the next within the pole's reach.

Once the other seven two-man teams positioned around the front half of the ship had attached knives, they also began slicing through the kelp stalks.

The ripple that ran through the seaweed alerted the green mass to the human attack. It swiftly retaliated.

When he noticed the purple flower on one of the leaves below him unfurl its pointed dark petals, Pepijn paused his stalk cutting and watched the blossom within emerging. It was as strange as the rest of the kelp, long and thin, about three-fingers wide, with a dark red back and cream front. Protruding down its length were yellow filaments, curved, similar to the legs of a centipede, each tipped with a tiny translucent sphere. He switched his gaze to the cream-colored top of the flower when the tip split into four tendrils that displayed similar translucent globes to those on its body filaments. Both fascinated and wary of the weird blossom, Pepijn watched the wavering tendrils when the plant turned towards him. Though he could see no eyes adorning what he thought of as its head, he sensed it could see him and might be sizing him up as a suitable meal. A cold chill crept down his backbone when an orifice ringed with teeth opened in the tip.

Pepijn slashed the knife at the evil bloom when it shot forward, its body slithering out from the petals and stalk that had concealed it. The flower dodged around the weapon and lunged at one of the hands holding it. Pepijn screamed when teeth pierced his flesh. A flash of movement directed his pain-filled gaze to the side. Two stalks wavered like venomous serpents less than a foot away, and more were coming. He panicked when the nearest two lunged at him. He struggled to stand straight, but the carnivorous flower attached to his hand prevented him. When one stalk latched onto his cheek and the other his wrist, two more spurts of excruciating pain flooded through his system.

He frantically tried tugging his arm free from the flower's grasp, but like the stalks, it was stuck fast and wasn't about to let go. Useless to prevent what was happening, Pepijn watched the four head tendrils reach for the back of his hand. Once each touched skin, the globes on their tips melted. His skin bubbled and peeled. Small dark things flowed through the tendrils and into his hand, fresh sources of agony to add to his pain-wracked body.

When he felt the rope around his waist cut into his skin, he felt some hope of rescue. Guillermo had finally realized something was amiss and hauled on it. He strained to help, but it was useless. More tendrils had attached themselves or wrapped around his arms, and all heaved him towards the waves. Almost caressingly, a stem slithered around his neck. When the strangling tightness he expected didn't come, Pepijn knew they had a different, less swift demise planned for him. There was only one direction he would be heading now, down into the cold sea and the hellish weed waiting to feed upon him like they had the dolphins. Picturing a long, painful death, he gazed at the waves. Though something he thought he would never wish for, drowning now seemed an altogether more pleasant way to die.

When the carnivorous plant released its hold, Pepijn shifted his terrified gaze to the intense burning sensation emanating from the four patches of blistered skin on his hand and the bloody red welt in the center. His screams increased when small versions of the plant that had sown its seeds inside him sprouted from his hand and halfway up his arm.

Barely hearing Pepijn's screams above the plethora of sounds around him, Guillermo pulled on the rope when the attached man began to struggle. Confused as to why he couldn't haul him up, he kept a tight grip as he moved to the rail. Guillermo gasped at the sight of the stalks attached and wrapped around his friend. He saw the strange flower looking up at him with blood around its gaping mouth staining its ring of sharp, barbed teeth. Guillermo released the rope as something pulled it through his grip with such force and speed; it burned his skin. Screaming, Pepijn splashed onto the blanket of kelp. Guillermo unhooked the lantern from the rail and aimed it at his friend being passed across the vicious kelp by the stalks. Shocked by what he witnessed, Guillermo turned away when his friend disappeared into the darkness, and his screams were carried away by the wind. His gaze around the ship picked out other teams experiencing the kelp's retaliation. He headed for the nearest to see if he could help.

Standing on the quarterdeck, Fokke had observed the teams' failed attempts to rid the ship of the kelp by pulling free the stalks. His disposition improved when knives were brought into play to sever their hold on his ship. Cutting them loose was the solution. Then the carnage began. He stared in disbelief at the kelp attacking the men leaning over the side. Just when he thought it couldn't get any worse, stalks shot over and latched onto two unfortunate men near the rail and yanked them overboard before anyone could react. As quickly as it had started, the attack was over.

Though he knew he should do something, the incident was so far outside his realm of normality; he was at a loss at what that should be. Instead, he observed the crew that had survived the unexpected onslaught draw knives and retreat from the rails, their eyes dancing nervously to every creak and movement around them. The boatswain rushing onto the quarterdeck shook him from his trance. He turned to the ashen-faced man, and for the first time in the twelve years that he had known the boatswain, he saw fear in his eyes.

"How many did we lose?" asked Fokke.

"Nine," answered Jozef. "The kelp's thicker aft and has climbed higher. It grabbed two of the crew by the rail and dragged them over."

"I saw that," replied Fokke, the scene replaying in his head. "Dead, I suppose."

Jozef nodded. "Even if they're alive, they won't be for long, and we can't launch a boat in this storm and with...*that* down there.

If they can reach us up here, they'll have no trouble attacking a boat."

"What do we do now?" asked Drasbart, joining them. He was as unnerved as everyone else onboard who had witnessed the carnage. "If we can't cut it off, how do we free ourselves from its grasp?"

He received no reply.

"What I find strange is that they all attacked at the same time," said Jozef, "as if coordinated."

With creased brow, the captain looked at Jozef. "Are you implying the seaweed is intelligent?"

Jozef shrugged. "Maybe? It isn't normal; I know that. Seaweed doesn't eat meat or attack men and ships."

"That's as may be, but as we've just borne witness this stuff does." Fokke stroked his beard, a sure sign he was apprehensive. "That might not be our only problem. Those things on the leaves we thought were seed pods don't contain seeds but small, sleek creatures—vicious buggers. I caught one and have it sealed in a rum cask in my quarters."

Jozef groaned. "Could this voyage get any worse?" Glimpsing movement from the corner of his eye, Drasbart turned and gasped at the stalks slithering over the rail. "I think it just has."

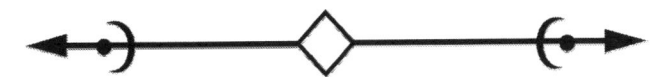

CHAPTER 5
Attacked and Repelled

After staring at the stalks for a few fearful moments, Fokke turned to the boatswain. "Grab men and axes, knives, anything we can fight them off with and bring them here." When the frightened boatswain failed to drag his eyes away from the boarding menace, he pushed the man into action. "Snap out of it, Jozef. The only way any of us are going to live through this is to repel them."

Brought back to his senses, Jozef ran a hand through his soaked hair to push it from his face and nodded. "Aye, Captain."

"We could use fire," offered Drasbart. "Make some torches with timber and pitch and drive them back with the flames."

Fokke quickly considered the proposal. Usually, they guarded against fire, the enemy of a wooden ship, but desperate times call for desperate measures, and their situation was dire. The deck was soaked with spray and rain so if they were careful; the torches might save them. "Jozef, also have the carpenter fashion torches while the rest of us fight them off as best we can."

Jozef leaped down the stairs and started shouting orders to the drenched and anxious crew.

Fokke refocused on the menacing vines now lining the rear third of the quarterdeck. Uncannily snakelike, they undulated in the air with their sucker tips looking at them. Though the wind had waned slightly and along with it the powerful swells that had rocked the ship precariously, the storm still had them in its grasp. Rain thrummed on the decks and streamed down the slim vines.

"I wonder why they've stopped," pondered Fokke aloud.

Maybe they've reached their growth limit," suggested Drasbart.

"Or they're waiting for something?" uttered Fokke ominously.

Hurried footsteps on the stairs turned their heads to the men rushing up them. All brandished a weapon of some type suitable for repelling the carnivorous weed. These included axes; swords; knives, some long and pointed; a meat cleaver borrowed from the galley kitchen; and lumps of wood as makeshift cudgels.

On spying the stalks that turned their sucker heads in their direction, the men advanced cautiously.

Eager to have revenge for what they did to his friend, Guillermo was the first to attack. The axe he swung sliced through a stalk and chipped a large fragment from the top rail. While the severed tip flopped to the deck and convulsed before going still, the other part flapped about wildly, slinging dark ooze from the cut. Witnessing Guillermo killing one of the intimidating vines so easily boosted their confidence, and bravado led the rest of the men to attack. Their punishment upon the stalks was swift and brutal. They sliced, stabbed and bashed them into submission, covering the deck with their dark blood-sap. As the severed end of the stalks retreated over the rail, more appeared to replace them. Goaded by their success, the men made swift work of them also.

"It's working," exclaimed Drasbart triumphantly.

Fokke, less reassured, nodded weakly and turned to survey the rest of his ship. He was pleased to see Jozef had set up sentries around the rails to warn of an attack from other directions where, oddly, none was forthcoming. It worried him that the weed only attacked in one place. It was as if it were testing their defenses. Surely it couldn't be that intelligent?

The boatswain crossed to the carpenter who had appeared on deck carrying an armful of staves tipped with pitch-soaked rope and cloth. After a few had been handed out to the mid-deck sentries, who were prepared to light them from lanterns placed nearby if danger threatened, Jozef brought the rest of them up to the quarterdeck while the carpenter went to fashion more.

Fokke returned his attention to the men fighting the weed behind him when one screamed. The man responsible for the cry had been accidentally barged by another who had lurched forward with a sword to decapitate the sucker end of a stalk. Slipping on the deck slick with sap-blood, he crashed into the rail, his face staring down at the monstrous kelp creeping up the hull. Seizing their chance of easy prey; three of the stalks attacked. The first shot at the man's face and attached its sucker to his eye, digging in its teeth, and wrenching it from its socket, snapping the optic nerve.

Screaming in agony, its victim swung the sword at the vine responsible. The second stalk wrapped around the man's weapon hand and constricted as powerfully as any python. The sword clattered to the deck as the third vine wrapped around the man's neck.

Noticing the man in trouble, Guillermo chopped at another stalk and rushed to his aid, but the man was dragged over the rail before he reached him. Guillermo risked a peek over the side. In the gloom that surrounded the ship, he glimpsed the stricken man being passed along the kelp just as Pepijn had been. He spun to attack when something nudged him.

"Steady on, shipmate," exclaimed Pieter, dodging away from the raised axe aimed at his head. "Grab yerself one of these."

Guillermo glanced at the torch Pieter held. Flames and black smoke drifted from it fanned by the wind and hissed when the rain struck. When Pieter turned away and began thrusting the fiery weapon at the stalks, Guillermo swung the axe, embedding it in the rail for quick retrieval if required, and went to get a torch of his own.

While Drasbart held open the door of a lantern, Jozef lit the torches and handed them out to the men. With the wooden staves being almost as tall as a man, they could keep a safe distance as they thrust them at the stalks. After a few of the vines had suffered scorching, the others swiftly slithered back over the rail in retreat.

"That worked better than I expected," said Drasbart.

"The torches were a fine idea of yours." Jozef slapped a heavily calloused hand on the first mate's shoulder. "Hopefully they've learned their lesson and won't be back."

"I don't think that's something we can rely on while they still have hold of the ship," said Fokke, pondering their next move.

"They retreat from heat, so we could try driving them away from the hull with the flames, Captain," suggested Drasbart.

Fokke shook his head. "It's too risky. I've already lost too many men. A few more and we'll be hard pushed to work the ship."

To save on costs that would reduce his profit, Fokke always sailed with a skeleton crew plus a few extras to allow for the loss from shipboard hazards. Scurvy and a fall from the rigging had claimed three deaths on the outward journey, eating into his reserves, leaving him a crew of forty-nine plus his first mate and himself. "The stalks are too many and move so fast they'll either pull the torches from the men's grasps or drag them over to their doom. No, we wait and see what the damn weed will do next. In the meantime, we come up with a more permanent solution to rid us of this green menace."

Without any conviction of its success, Fokke glanced up at the heavens as he mouthed a silent prayer asking for salvation for himself, his crew, and his ship from the menace that threatened them all.

Prepared to fend off another attack if it came, the men remained alert as they waited and wondered if any of them would be alive by daybreak.

CHAPTER 6

Strategy

As the night lengthened, the storm abated, leaving the ship rolling gently on rough seas yet to calm from its passing. The rain, though, continued to fall heavily, causing the few members of the crew lucky enough to have waterproof jackets to be thankful they had committed to the expense. Those who weren't so astute or as prosperous wore the usual seafarers' attire of woolen and canvas garments that failed to keep the wet and cold from seeping through to their skin. Clothes leaden from the constant drenching they received on the exposed deck, they cursed the foul weather. Though wet, uncomfortable and wishing they were anywhere other than on the accursed, rain-battered vessel, they remained alert as they paced back and forth in a lame attempt to ward off the shivering chill that wrapped them in its cold embrace.

After two hours of inactivity from the omnipresent threat and aware the men would be useless if they didn't rest, Fokke sent

Hell Ship

half his crew below to eat and sleep while the rest remained on watch. After the below deck crew had eaten, the ship's cook brought those above a tot of rum and a large pot of warm food with bowls they could dip into it while they remained on duty, eating where they stood.

Fokke, Drasbart, and Jozef went to the captain's quarters to grab some food and discuss the situation. They knew they needed to come up with a plan to rid themselves of the malicious weed they suspected would soon launch another attack more ferocious than the last.

As Tom brought their meals from the galley to the cabin and served it and drinks to the officers, they ran through a few ideas that might see them free of the weed.

After discussing and discounting any ideas with little chance of accomplishing the desired outcome, they decided on two possible plans of action. Though both had faults, both had different probabilities of success. The first to be considered involved hoisting full sail and trying to drag themselves free of the weed while men used torches to dislodge as many of the stalks as they could. The second involved pouring boiling pitch on the kelp attached to the ship and setting light to it. After some discussion, they finally decided on a combination of the two with changes.

As the blazing torches had revealed, the kelp retreated from heat, but having men lean over the side for the stems to grab was too risky, and lighting pitch so close to the hull was extremely hazardous to the ship. They decided they would use boiling water instead, and at the same time as pouring the scalding water in a coordinated attack around the hull onto the weed, they would hoist the sails to pull them free before the plants could latch on again.

Drasbart unsuccessfully stifled a yawn. It had been a long, harrowing day for them all. "I believe our plan has a high chance of victory."

"I hope so," said Fokke, "as I don't know what else we can do to rid ourselves of it if it fails."

"Probably best we wait until daylight to do it," said Drasbart. "The storm has practically passed us by and should be gone by morning. Carrying pots of boiling water around in the dark with the current roll of the ship could prove hazardous."

"Makes sense to me," agreed Jozef. "It'll also give the crew presently on watch a chance to rest."

"I also approve," said Fokke, pleased they soon might be free of the menacing plant life. He turned to Jozef. "Roust the men below and have them change shift with those up top. Then you two get some sleep. I'll take first watch, and one of you can swap with me in two hours and then swap with the other two hours after that. If danger threatens, ring the bell."

Pleased with their strategy, the three men exited the cabin, leaving Tom to clear away the dinner things.

CHAPTER 7

They Come. They Kill.

After biding its time, as if aware the humans aboard the ship would become weary and less alert as the night deepened, a ripple of activity spread across the kelp. Groups of sleek and crab-like creatures ranging from cat-size to the size of medium-size dogs, all vicious and hungry, emerged from underwater nests formed by leaves entwined below the surface. They scampered onto the carpet of kelp, their clawed limbs carrying them towards the unsuspecting ship. On reaching the hull, they clambered up the side.

Sheltering the bowl of his pipe with a cupped palm, Yannick dragged a lungful of the strong tobacco-scented smoke into his lungs, the glowing embers briefly giving warmth to his cold hand. He exhaled with satisfaction, the breeze whisking away the stream of smoke as he glanced over at Jaap who was wrapping a strip of oiled canvas around the bulbous bundle of pitch-soaked rope and rag on the stave tip to keep it dry.

Yannick's gaze around the gloomy decks picked out his fellow rain-lashed shipmates, all vigilant for another attack from the mysterious seaweed, and the first mate on the quarterdeck. Highlighted in the lantern light, Drasbart stood erect, hands behind his back, peering the length of the ship with a worried frown.

As Yannick wondered where the killer kelp had hailed from, he failed to notice the head of the sleek creature appear over the rail. After surveying the other crew dispersed along the deck, it focused its malicious eyes on him.

The sleek wolf-size creature was the patriarch; commanding both species that had made the kelp mass their home, receiving its protection in return for food. The tentacles on the back of the larger, more ruthless, and wiser creature were directed at the nearest human as he anticipated his fill. It turned its head each way along the side of the ship before focusing on the opposite rail where more of its pack, waiting for the order to attack, clung to the ship's hull out of sight of the humans. Raising its head, it stretched out its neck, opened its jaws and directed a high-pitched squeal around the ship. As its vicious army appeared over the rails, the patriarch turned away and headed back to its underwater nest.

Barely audible to human ears, Yannick felt the creature's battle cry more than heard it. Confused by the painful sensation in his ears that dissipated as swiftly as it had arrived, he turned his head to the rail and gasped in fear at the creatures scuttling over the side in an insidious wave of horror and death. The pipe fell from his lips when he shouted a warning to his shipmates. He snatched the canvas covering from the torch gripped in his shaking hand, pulled open the door of the lantern hanging from the mainmast and thrust the end into the wind-flickered flame. The flammable pitch ignited with a satisfying whoosh of heat. He jerked in pain when something small landed on his back and dug in its claws. Yannick spun and swept the blazing torch at the surrounding creatures moving in on him and slammed his back into the mast, crushing the one that had attacked. Relieved to see them backing away from the flame, he stabbed the torch to drive them back over the side.

Yannick flicked his gaze at the patches of yellow light cast by the flaming torches his crewmates jabbed and swung at the creatures, highlighting the terrible swarm that almost covered the outer edges of the deck. He kicked out when something bit his leg and thrust the torch at the creature attached to his shin. The squealing beast released its grip and dropped to the deck. A stamp from his foot crunched it into a splatted mess. He arched his back and screamed when three leaped onto his back. While two of them shredded his clothes and skin with their talons, the third climbed onto his shoulder and stabbed its two front claws repeatedly into his neck. Blood poured from the wounds and changed Yannick's scream into a gurgled choking that sprayed blood from his mouth. Dropping the torch, he fell to his knees and toppled to the deck. Wishing death would mercifully claim him and end his pain, he tried to scream when one of the creatures raised its two long arms and stabbed claws down at his face.

Though Yannick still lived, the creatures moved away to search for another victim. Stalks waiting nearby snaked over the rail, wrapped around the dying man's ankles and whisked him over the side.

Ensuring they remained vigilant and prepared to repel another attack if it came, Drasbart was gazing at the anxious crew when it arrived. Scratching at an ear that tingled, he noticed the men tense, some stepping back as if thumped in the chest. Only when torches blazed into flame did he comprehend the terrifying cause. What seemed to be hundreds of creatures ranging in size and form swarmed over the sides of the ship and attacked the men. A couple of the sleeker, scale-covered creatures were paler and bloated with shapes of the large eggs they nurtured within pregnant bellies. The other species were more crab-like with bulbous, octopus-like bodies of varying shades of green mottled with patches of uneven brown spots. They had six strangely placed limbs; three on its abdomen ending in a single claw-spike, one in the middle at the front adorned with two claws, and two long spindly arm appendages attached to the sides of its body. Protruding from the front was a head that could be extended and retracted like a turtle's. Its beak-like jaw split into four sections when it opened to snap at its victims. Above the jaw were two black eyes with bright white centers.

One man, slow to react, was overpowered by creatures as he scrambled to light his torch. The unlit torch dropped from his hands when he thudded to the deck, his body immediately smothered with the vicious fiends that ripped and stabbed at his writhing body.

Drasbart's terrified gaze at the many battles spread around the ship revealed more men suffering horribly from the onslaught. Recovering from his shock, he crossed to the bell and furiously rung it.

At the sound of the bell, some of the crew eating in the galley abandoned their meals and rushed along the corridor. Others, rousted from their slumber by the warning signal alerting them of an attack, slipped from their hammocks and joined their comrades hurrying along the corridor.

Tom, also alerted by the insistent clangs, crawled from his makeshift bed beneath the steps leading up to the deck, grabbed one of the unlit torches leaning against the wall and lit it from the nearby lantern as footsteps rushed towards him. He handed a blazing torch to each man who passed and sped up the steps.

When the men from below poured onto the deck, Drasbart ceased his bell ringing. He watched the men spread out in a fan shape and begin thrusting the flaming tips of their torches at the creatures around them. It was a tactic they had discussed if another attack was forthcoming. The sounds of the creatures' pained screeches drifted down to Tom. Having completed his duty, he closed the lantern door and cautiously climbed the steps armed with a flaming torch of his own. His gaze around at the crew fighting the creatures picked out the first mate rushing towards him. Tom dodged around the men and sprinted up to the quarterdeck.

Drasbart took the torch from Tom. "Go inform the captain of what's happening. If he's asleep, wake him!"

Tom nodded and rushed off to carry out the order.

At the bow, Olaf and Johan were in trouble. Back to back, they swiped and thrust their torches at the evil beasts encircling them. Johan glanced behind at the creatures; they would be ripped to shreds if they attacked from all directions. Aware there were too many for the two of them to hold at bay for much longer, his frightened gaze searched for an escape route and halted on the foremast rigging a few steps away; it was their only chance. He tilted his head at Olaf as he swept the fiery brand back and forth low to the deck. "Climb the rigging," he shouted.

Olaf, his face masked in fear, nodded, threw his torch at the nearest creatures and sprinted for the rigging with Johan beside him. They both leaped onto the rail, grabbed the soaked rope and began climbing. Their attackers followed.

Johan glanced down at the nightmare things scrambling up the rope netting, and though aware they were backing themselves into a corner, they continued climbing, prolonging the inevitable. As one, the two men jumped onto the yardarm and balanced precariously on the narrow rain-slicked platform that swayed and creaked with the movements of the ship. They gripped the leach-lines to prevent themselves from being thrown off and directed their terrified gazes at the climbing menace. Both drew their knives. They wouldn't go down without a fight.

The first creature to climb onto the yardarm was swiftly sent flying by a kick from Olaf. The second one he kicked at stabbed a limb into his bare foot. With adrenalin damping the pain, he shook his foot vigorously to free it, but it latched on with more claws that dug into his shin and began climbing up his leg, ripping deep gashes with each clawed purchase. Three more leaped onto him and climbed toward his chest, leaving behind a trail of puncture marks that seeped blood into his soaked clothing.

Johan was fighting his own battles, kicking off those that climbed onto the yardarm and swiping the sharp blade at those that leaped at him. Terrified he was about to be overpowered, he kicked and stabbed at any within reach, put the knife between his teeth and climbed to the crow's nest.

He scrambled inside and gazed down as the creatures climbed onto the yardarm. While some joined the attack on Olaf, the remainder climbed the mast, shrouds, and rigging. Johan watched his friend stab frantically at those on his body with his knife, stabbing himself in the process. Olaf released his hold on the rope to pull a creature from his face. Slippery with rain and blood, his foot slipped from the yardarm, sending him toppling below.

Johan's gaze followed the man's fall until he crashed to the deck, crushing some of the creatures that had continued slashing his flesh during the fall. Returning his focus to his desperate plight, Johan knew he was defeated. To delay the inevitable when the creatures reached the crow's nest, he climbed to the fore royal yardarm.

His gaze picked out the battles of the crew far below highlighted in patches of lantern light. The reinforcements from below deck seemed to be driving the creatures toward the rail. With nowhere to go except down, Johan switched his gaze to the cold sea where the weed thinned out nearer the bow. If he leaped from the end of the yardarm, he should be able to clear it enabling him to swim to the forward man-overboard line, one of three knotted ropes hanging at intervals along each side of the ship, climb back on board and help his shipmates drive the creatures away.

It was a perilous strategy, made more dangerous by the murderous kelp, but at least it offered him a slim chance of survival which was currently zero by remaining where he was. He stamped on a creature when it climbed onto his precarious perch, slipped his knife into the sheath at his waist and ran along the yardarm. Murmuring a prayer for salvation, he dived from the end.

As the icy sea shockingly embraced him, Johan gasped; almost exhaling the lungful of precious air collected on his way down. To halt the force of the long drop hurtling him towards the seabed, he flapped his arms frantically. As his descent slowed, he gazed around at the kelp barely an arm's length away. What they had seen from the surface was only a fraction of what lay beneath. It was about six feet thick and dotted with leaf-entwined bulges with dark, uninviting apertures. He saw a few much larger leaf bulges with equally larger openings, scattered over the vast leafy mass.

Thick stalks with large round leaves on the tips hung below the dense mass of weed and moved back and forth. Though the leaves were spread out on the forward stroke to push against the water, they turned sideways to glide through the water on the return, like an oarsman feathering the oars to reduce resistance.

Johan realized the significance of what he witnessed. *The stalks were rowing backward. It was why the Fortuyn failed to make any headway. Though they suspected the weight of the weed was holding them back, none of them had envisioned this.*

Long stems stretched under the hull and held on like limpets, cradling the ship in its grasp. Noticing a different color amongst the dark mass, Johan focused in on it. Sucker tentacles attached to the pale, sea-wrinkled object throbbed as if sucking something through them. When it turned with the current to face him, Johan recognized what it was—a man. Though difficult to tell in this light and at this distance, he thought it might be Pepijn, one of the crewmen the weed had grabbed from the ship. The plant was feeding on him.

Feeling his air running out, Johan was about to swim to the surface when he saw something slide from the mass in front of him; it was Yannick, hanging upside down from tentacles gripping his ankles. His eyeballs, attached only by their optic nerves, drifted across his lifeless torn face. Air bubbled from Johan's screaming mouth. He swam to the surface and burst above the waves. He gulped down air and turned to the ship. Bursts of yellow light dancing above the deck indicated the battle still raged. Along its length, stalks dragged men, both alive, dead and some state in between, over the rails as nourishment for the sinister kelp.

Johan swam for the knotted rope hanging down the side of the ship and gripped the end trailing in the water. As he pulled himself along its length, something burst from the water beside him—a sucker stalk. Three more rapidly appeared and focused their tips on him. For a moment, man and plant stared at one another.

Beneath the surface, Johan drew his knife. When one of the stalks lunged at his face, he swiped the blade at it, slicing clean through. His backward slice saw another sucker severed. As if receiving a plea for help, stalks appeared around him. He slashed out with the blade, severing five more before one grabbed his wrist. He bit down on the tendril, ripped it free and spat out the foul plant chunk.

When something slithered around his ankles, he knew what was coming and took deep breaths before they pulled him below the surface. The stalks that held him hauled him under their mass and stopped by a thick bundle of leaves much larger than the others. Suspecting something horrific dwelled within, Johan peered through the opening into its dark interior. Two eyes blinked open. Red, bright and menacing, they stared at him. When the points of light moved closer, and the terrifying thing emerged, Johan put the knife to his own throat, pressed hard and slid it across his skin. Redness filled his vision, and through the bloody haze, he glimpsed the eyes closing in and monstrous jaws stretching wide to receive him. He welcomed the quick death that ended the unimaginable horror that was about to befall him.

◇

Woken from his fitful slumber by the furiously ringing bell, Fokke sat up and shook the fatigued fuzziness from his brain. Having slept fully clothed in case of an emergency, he pulled on his boots and glanced at the bedchamber door when glass tinkled to the floorboards. His worried gaze fixated on the snakelike shadows moving through the wardroom's lantern light cast on the floor. He cocked an ear to the sound of something scurrying across floorboards and grabbed the loaded flintlock pistol he had placed beside his bed before resting. He crept to the door and peered around the frame into his wardroom.

He saw the smashed gallery window, and the two sucker stalks, and huge creature, four times the size of the egg creature he had captured, were inside. They seemed to be searching for something. Muffled movement from within the sea chest turned the stalk heads to it, and the giant creature scampered over and climbed onto it. It tapped a claw on the lid a few times and waited. Muffled taps answered. It turned its head to the waiting stalks, screeched a series of drawn-out clicks and jumped to the floor when the plant appendages moved to the sea chest.

The stalks' efforts to force their way between the lid joint were thwarted by the two clasps holding it closed. Assuming they were here to rescue the captured creature—a loss Fokke now welcomed—he elected to remain hidden and silent in the hope they would give up and leave.

Not to be outwitted, the stalks moved around the sides of the large chest. While one paused at a hinge to examine it, the other arrived at a clasp. After studying and prodding it a few times, it seemed to have worked out it might be the thing preventing them from getting inside. It turned to the observing creature nearby and prodded its sucker at the clasp.

Both fascinated and concerned by the carnivorous plant's level of intelligence, Fokke observed the creature stab at the clasp with a claw and then hook it under and release it. After the stalk had examined the open clip, it moved to the second one and tapped it. The creature scuttled along to it and hooked it open. They both forced their tips between the join and raised the lid.

The creature climbed inside and screeched to its captive brethren, touching claws with the one that was poking through the air hole of the small cask. The two stalks reached inside and after examining all sides of the object, lifted it out and smashed it against the floor until it splintered. The trapped creature clawed at the break until it had made a big enough hole to escape through. Like parent and child reunited, they nuzzled together for a moment before heading for the broken window.

Thankful they were leaving, Fokke watched the two creatures dive through the broken window and waited for the stalks to follow them. An urgent knock upon the door halted them by the window. Fokke turned his head to the door when the cabin boy spoke.

"Captain, Mr. Drasbart requests yer urgent attention upon deck. Hundreds of creatures are attacking."

Fokke cursed the boy's untimely arrival. A few more seconds and he would have been safe. Choosing not to acknowledge the boy's presence in the hope he and the stalks would leave, Fokke waited.

In the corridor, Tom put his ear to the door to detect any sounds that would reveal the captain had heard him and was stirring. Hearing only the normal sounds of the ship at sea, he rapped harder on the door. "Captain, the creatures are attacking again, and Mr. Drasbart requests yer urgent presence topside."

When no reply from his captain was forthcoming, Tom decided to enter and rouse Fokke from his slumber. The first mate's order was to alert the captain of the danger, and he wasn't going to fail him. He turned the handle and opened the door.

Fokke sighed when the handle turned and flicked his gaze to the clacking at the window as two of the smaller crab-like creatures entered. It seemed the stalks had called for reinforcements. The two plant tendrils slithered across the room and stretched towards the door, while the two animals climbed the walls and moved along the ceiling to drop on anyone who entered.

To save the boy, he would have to reveal himself. His eyes glanced at his sword hanging on the wall across the room. With only one shot in the pistol, it was his only chance to save them both. He raised the weapon, darted into the room and fired at the nearest creature. The lead ball almost severed its head from its body. It dropped to the floor and wriggled as life left it. As the stalk lunged at him, Fokke flipped the pistol over to use as a club and smashed at the stem with enough force to send it crashing into the wall. He ducked under the second tendril and slammed a shoulder into the half-open door, sending Tom staggering backward into the passage and smashing into the opposite wall. He threw the pistol at the second creature but missed when it sprung to the floor. Two strides brought him to his sword. He snatched it from the wall, and with no time to pull it from its sheath, swung it at the stalk shooting at his face, knocking it to the side. Dodging the creature's attack at his leg, he flicked the casing from the blade, sending it flying across the room. The sheath struck another crab creature climbing in and knocked it back through the window. Fokke raised the sword at the two attacking stalks. A broad sweep of the weapon cut through them both. Before their severed tips touched the floor, he stabbed the tip into the creature scurrying across the floor towards him. He raised the sword and stared at the impaled fiend trying to wriggle free while it swiped claws at him. Lowering the sword, he slid the creature off with his foot and crunched and ground its exoskeleton into the floorboards.

Knocking on the door, Tom called out, "Captain, are yer okay? Do yer need assistance?"

"I'm fine, lad," replied Fokke, turning his head to something scraping on the window.

It seemed the creature's cries or the plant's distress had brought forth further reinforcements. As more of the plant limbs and animals smashed through the glass panes, Fokke collected his pistol from the floor, exited his cabin and closed the door.

Shoving the pistol into his waistband, Fokke looked at Tom. "Come on, lad, let's go give some assistance to those battling topside."

"Aye, sir." Tom followed the captain as he walked briskly along the corridor.

As Fokke stepped onto the deck, he stamped on one creature, grabbed another from the air that jumped at his face and smashed it into the quarterdeck wall, spraying Tom with its foul blood, and gazed around his crew's ongoing battles.

A group of men who had formed a semicircle had successfully driven a large group of the creatures back to the rail. Jabs of their torches sent some fleeing over the side. A short distance along the deck, a screaming sailor, blood dripping from the many wounds over his body and face, was hoisted into the air by the vines and disappeared over the edge of the ship. The only good news was that the wind had dropped, and the rain was now little more than a gentle shower.

Fokke glanced at the cabin boy behind him. "Stick close to me, lad."

Tom nodded and followed the captain across the deck to the steps leading up to the quarterdeck. Fokke slashed, stabbed and crushed any of the creatures in his path. Tom snatched up an abandoned torch, its long handle covered in blood, both human and animal, and jabbed and swung it at the beasts looking for a meal, driving them back. When they reached the short flight of steps, the captain rushed up them. Tom remained at the bottom, swinging the flames at any creatures that came within reach.

On the quarterdeck, the first mate and three crew had successfully driven their attackers to the rail. A few jabs of the flames each wielded sent the creatures diving over the side screeching from their burns.

The first officer turned as the captain reached the top of the steps and joined him in gazing along the ship. They seemed to be winning the battle. The creatures' crushed and burnt bodies now littered the deck, and those that remained were being forced back by the flames.

"I think we've got the better of them now, sir," said Drasbart.

"But at what cost?" frowned Fokke, scraping his sword blade on the rail to remove the creatures' blood.

Drasbart gazed around at the survivors. "Difficult to say until we do an exact tally, but we must have lost at least twenty men.

Fokke cursed the creatures. "It's imperative that we free ourselves of this deadly menace before we lose more souls."

Drasbart was in total agreement. "As soon as there's a break in the fighting, I'll have the men start boiling water and setting sail to pull us clear."

Fokke turned to the three men guarding the quarterdeck rail against a fresh incursion. "Raf, you're to remain here to protect our rear. You other two are with us." He turned back to his first mate. "It's time we reclaimed our ship."

Drasbart nodded. "Amen to that."

Fokke swapped his sword for Tom's torch and ordered him up to the quarterdeck to assist Raf in guarding the stern.

The four men spread out. As they slowly moved toward the bow, they thrust the torches at the creatures, driving them back. When they reached other members of the crew involved in their battles, they helped them defeat the beasts they were fighting before moving on. Leaving men at intervals to guard the rails they had cleared, they assembled all available crew to join their line.

As they scuttled backward to avoid the burning flames, the creatures failed to realize that the humans were herding them.

Noticing the success of the captain's line, Jozef, busy fighting at the bow, rallied those around him into a similar formation and drove the creatures towards the stern. When the two groups of animals met, the men encircled them and stabbed the flames at them. The creatures' high-pitched squeals filled the air tainted with the stench of their burning flesh.

When the last one had succumbed to the flames, a deathly silence reigned on the ship. The rain ceased, and the breeze grew gentle, the creaks of the vessel welcome normality.

A shriek, long and menacing, came from the sea on the port side. Splashes, unnatural footsteps on water, approached the ship and cast the men's anxious gazes to the port rail.

The captain strode to the side and stared into the darkness at the approaching sounds. Whatever was coming was concealed by the night's lightless cloak. He drew the long-handled torch back like a spear and let it fly. Before the sea extinguished its tip, he glimpsed something substantial, evil, and murderous moving purposefully for the ship across the weed. The creature raised its head and looked at him. Stunned by the terrible red-eyed monster he had caught sight of, Fokke backed away from the rail.

"What is it?" asked Jozef, his anxiousness increased by the captain's pale, terrified expression.

Fokke turned his head to the boatswain. "Something new. A large hell-spawned demon."

Clacks on the hull caused by something climbing up the ship sent fearful dread coursing through everyone trapped on board.

CHAPTER 8

The Final Skirmish

"What do we do, Captain?" asked Noah shakily, as he and his shipmates gazed in fright in the direction of the approaching clicks.

Snapping out of his fright, Fokke glanced around at his scared crew. "Use your torches to stop it boarding and send it back to Hell!" He turned to his first mate, fished a key from his pocket and handed it and his empty pistol to Drasbart. "Take two men and Tom to the arms locker. When you've loaded a few, send Tom topside to hand them out."

"Aye, sir." Drasbart selected the two nearest men and headed below deck, calling Tom to join them on the way.

The boatswain ushered the reluctant men nearer the port side with threats of a lashing if any deserted their post. Though some of the men believed a lashing would be preferable to what they were about to face, they all aimed the torches gripped in their sweating, trembling hands at where they thought the latest threat on what had turned out to be a nightmare voyage, would appear.

When a clawed limb covered in tiny scales that shimmered in the torchlight appeared over the side, its talons gripped the rail with enough force to splinter the wood. A gasp of fear rippled through the men staring at the webbed claw. Tips of tentacles rose into view and directed their heads over the frightened humans.

"Hold!" ordered the captain sternly when a couple of men went to step back.

The clacking on the hull had ceased with the appearance of the limb. It had stopped. It was waiting.

The boatswain leaned towards the captain. "Why do you think it stopped?"

Fokke shrugged. "How the hell should I know?"

Seizing his chance to wound this new monstrosity to threaten his ship and crew, Fokke snatched a cutlass from the man beside him and pushed through the line of men. He cautiously approached the leg, and halting an arm's length away, he raised the sword and swung it at the limb with all his vengeful might.

A terrible shriek rang out when the blade sliced the scaly limb. The patriarch creature, keen to taste more human flesh and to show its weaker brethren how to defeat the humans, leaped over the side, avoiding a second swing of the sword by a hair's breadth. It jumped onto the mizzenmast rigging and swiped a claw-tipped rear leg at the men nearby. A deep gash opened across one man's chest, the other man dropped his torch and grasped hands at his neck. Blood poured through his fingers.

The nearest crew thrust torches at the monstrosity, sending it scampering higher until the darkness concealed it. With their fearful gazes raised aloft for the giant beast, the men held their torches ready to fend off its expected attack.

As the man with the sliced throat collapsed to the ground and gurgled his last breaths, the boatswain ordered the man with the gashed chest to head below to get it seen to by the ship's surgeon.

Tom appeared on deck carrying an armful of weapons that included flintlock pistols of a variety of makes; four blunderbusses, excellent short-range funs to repel pirates; and a pistol axe the boatswain had won in a card game against a Polish sea captain. The boatswain intercepted Tom and quickly handed out the weapons.

Tom crossed to the captain and handed him back his pistol. "Loaded and ready to fire, Captain."

Without taking his eyes from the rigging, Fokke took the pistol.

Tom followed his gaze to the gloomy upper half of the mizzenmast, where he assumed the creature the first mate had said was coming now hid.

Tom tapped the waterproof munitions bag hanging from his shoulder. "I have spare cartridges, powder and shot ready to reload."

"Good lad," commended the Captain, who sensed they would need them. He took the bag and handed it to Guillermo nearby. "Return to the quarterdeck."

"Aye, sir." Tom returned to the quarterdeck.

After a few minutes of inactivity, which was more nerve-wracking than an attack, Fokke turned to a man armed with a blunderbuss. It had a limited range, but it wasn't accuracy he was after. "Noah, fire a shot up the mast to see if we can flush it down."

"Aye, Captain." Noah pointed the weapon skywards, rested the wooden stock against his shoulder, and pulled the trigger.

The explosive flash shed some brief light on the upper rigging and picked out the monstrous creature perched on the top yardarm peering down at them. Tentacles covering its upper back wavered in the air. It screeched when lead shot peppered its hideous form. Reclaimed by the dark, the terrified sailors heard it bound along the yardarm and after a few moments of silence, a splash. It had jumped overboard.

The crew cheered their success and the fleeing of the monster.

"Hush, you fools," reprimanded the captain sternly.

The men's rejoicing promptly faded.

Footsteps broke the dreaded silence that had befallen the deck. The first mate and the two crewmen who had accompanied him crossed to the men and quietly handed out the variety of loaded flintlock weapons they carried to those without one.

Crossing to Guillermo, Noah grabbed what he needed from the ammo bag and reloaded.

All eyes anxiously swept the sides of the ship for signs of the creature's return.

The creaks of the ship, thrumming of lines, and the gentle splash of waves on the hull were the only sounds to penetrate the eerie silence.

Slithering sounds turned the nervous men's frightened gazes to starboard and the tentacles rising above the rail, sinuously oscillating like evil serpents studying their prey as each prepared to strike.

"Get ready men, but wait for my signal," whispered Drasbart, barely loud enough for all the crew to hear.

Those that had firearms cocked the firing mechanisms and aimed them at the writhing menace. The men armed with flaming torches held them ready to thrust at the plant when it attacked.

The creatures' patriarch, recently forced to abandon the ship, headed for the hull. Water streamed from its body when it stealthily climbed the port side. It peered over the rail at the humans distracted by the writhing stalks, their unprotected backs ideal targets for its viciousness. It crept its powerful limbs over the side, and with claws retracted, it skulked closer to the unsuspecting humans.

Tom moved his weight from one foot to the other to force some circulation through them while he kept his eyes glued to the rail edge. He had only turned away briefly when the boom of a blunderbuss shattered the silence that had fallen on the ship. The following cheers from the crew made him believe that whatever they had shot at had suffered from the blast. He glanced at Raf, a veteran sailor and the oldest man on board, more gray, straggly beard than face, when he spat a globule of dark, mashed goo over the side and took yet another bite from his wedge of chewing tobacco. He paused in returning it to his pocket and held it out to Tom, who glanced at the recently bitten end, damp with the man's saliva and groove-marked from his rotten, gapped teeth, and shook his head. Raf shrugged, slipped it back in his pocket and again concentrated on the rail.

Wondering what was happening on the mid-deck, Tom shot a glance over the side to check it was clear and then looked back along the ship. He gasped at the sizeable sleek creature that crept up on the unsuspecting crew; their attention focused on the twisting line of tendrils along the starboard side.

When the creature hunched down on its four back limbs ready to spring, Tom cupped a hand to his mouth and yelled a warning. "Look out! It's behind you!"

Some of the crew turned their heads towards the shout and saw Tom frantically pointing at the port side. The patriarch ran claws down the backs of the first men it reached. They screamed.

Men turned to see the agonized expressions and arched backs of two of their comrades. The suffering men dropped their weapons and reached for the long rips of flapped open skin down their backs. The creature slammed into them, sending them reeling forwards into the others directly in front.

Flinching from the impact, one of the crew inadvertently tensed his finger on the trigger, blasting shot into the wounded man who had barged into him. The lead ball smashed through his shipmate's chin and exploded through teeth before lodging in the dying man's brain.

The man beside him raised his weapon at the monster and pulled the trigger. The creature swiped at the gun, knocking it aside as it went off. The shot entered another man's back, severing his spine and sending him flopping to the ground.

With his retreat blocked by those pressed behind, Noah thrust his torch at the creature's pointed face. The patriarch creature squealed as it dodged the flame and swiped out a claw, knocking it aside. It lurched forward, gripped Noah's head in its jaws and launched him at the other humans. As panic flowed through the crew, the creature speedily moved amongst them, ripping, biting and barging them aside in disarray. The tentacles on its back sought their own victims. Darting snakelike at any within reach, they tore chunks of flesh from their prey.

When Guillermo swept the flaming torch at the vicious tentacles, it focused the creature's swift vengeance upon him. Barely glimpsing the claw that swiped across his stomach before the monster turned away to attack another, he looked down and was horrified to witness his innards seeking to escape, forcing the deep gashes in his belly open. He dropped the torch and fell to his knees, clutching at his oozing guts to hold them in.

Unable to fire their weapons for fear of hitting their fellow shipmates, those around the outer edges moved away to seek a clear line of sight.

The patriarch swiped out a claw. Two men screamed as talons left deep gashes across their faces. Dodging back when the powerful creature attacked the man next to him, the boatswain aimed his pistol axe at the monster and fired. The shot grazed its side. The creature squealed and turned its murderous gaze upon him. Jozef lurched forward and swung the axe at its head. One of the creature's arm claws bit down on his wrist, halting the axe inches from its face. It twisted savagely. Bones crunched and broke. The pistol axe clattered as it fell. Its other front limb swiped at Jozef, knocking him to the ground with enough force to send him rolling along the deck. The creature chased him and stabbed a claw through his chest, ending his tumble-and his life.

Fokke pushed a man out of his way, raised his pistol at the creature and fired. The lead ball grazed the patriarch's head and smashed through the tip of one of the tentacles on its back.

Panicked shots fired by the terrified crew went wild of their erratic, ever-moving target and brought the monster's wrath down upon them.

The patriarch lunged at the nearest man and bit down on his arm. Crunching through skin, muscle, and bone, it drew its head back with the severed limb in its jaws. Flinging the gruesome prize at the group of four men backing away, it leaped upon them, biting, ripping and stabbing until all four were corpses.

As soon as he heard the first shot, Tom had rushed from the quarterdeck to assist.

Fokke called the boy to him and pointed at the powder bag. "Quick, Tom, powder and shot."

Tom crossed to Guillermo. Ignoring the dying man's pleas for help and the innards he was unsuccessfully trying to prevent spilling out from the large gashes in his stomach, he tugged the strap from the man's shoulder and returned to the captain.

As the captain reloaded, Tom rushed around to the other men handing out gunpowder and shot. He then collected the dropped weapons, moved to a safe distance and started reloading while the carnage continued.

"Those who have firearms," shouted the captain. Six men gathered around him. "Aim and fire at its head on my order." When all had their weapon trained on the creature continuing its carnage, Fokke shouted," Fire!"

Multiple shots rang out, sending lead at the creature and a cloud of acrid gray smoke forming around them. The creature's squeals indicated some of them had found their target. Fokke waved the smoke away and gazed at the dead and dying men, but there was no sign of the creature. He glanced at the crew around him. "Reload."

Tom rushed to them and swapped their discharged weapons with those he had reloaded before rushing off to reload them also.

With the screams and groans from his fallen crew ringing in his head, Fokke searched for the monster.

Luka Vanmulan, who had never been so terrified, wished his limbs would stop shaking as he directed the blunderbuss at the many shadows around him, any of which might be concealing the vicious demon. He put a hand to his head when something splattered on it and looked at the thick, dark liquid that stained his fingers. He shook it off and gazed up. Terror froze the scream on his lips when he saw the monster dropping from the yardarm. He panic-fired the weapon before he aimed, blasting the rail with shot. A stretched-out limb slashed across his face deep enough to scrape bone. Knocked to the ground by the creature landing on him, its claws digging deep into his flesh, Vanmulan screamed as he struck wildly at its head with the butt of the blunderbuss. The patriarch savagely ripped out the man's throat and, sprayed with the man's blood; it turned on those around it when one fired his pistol. It leaped when the lead ball grazed its shoulder and barged into three men, knocking them sprawling. A blunderbuss went off beside its head, deafening one ear. It ran a claw from the man's neck to his navel as it turned to another. He swiped away the pistol aimed at its face, deflecting the shot as it whizzed past its head. Burning powder singed its scales. It jumped on the man and bit off his face.

Shaking with terror, Wagner aimed the pistol at the creature that was close enough for him to breathe in its stagnant, briny stench. He pulled the trigger.

The patriarch screeched when another explosion rang out close by and pain burned in its side. It snarled at the human responsible, who reeked of fear.

Backing away, Wagner, his face masked with terror, threw the discharged weapon at the creature, turned and fled.

The patriarch bounded after the fleeing human and swiped at two men too sluggish to avoid its wrath. Both screamed from their painful wounds as they collapsed to the deck.

When the large creature set off in pursuit of Wagner, stalks snaked over the sides of the vessel and started dragging the dead, wounded and any human they came across off the ship to their feeding ground.

Casting a terrified glance behind at the monster in pursuit, Wagner headed for the forward door leading below deck and jumped down the steps. Landing awkwardly, almost twisting an ankle, he faltered before regaining his balance and rushing along the corridor.

Witnessing the monster's pursuit of Wagner, Fokke grasped his pistol hand with his other in an attempt to lessen its shaking, sighted on the animal and fired. Cursing when the shot missed and splintered the mast that the creature rushed past, he turned to survey the carnage left in its wake.

Geerhart fired his blunderbuss at three serpentine tentacles reaching for him. The blast shredded two, but the third whipped down at his leg and yanked him off his feet. Dragged towards the rail, he struck mercilessly at the frond wrapped around his ankle, doing more damage to his leg than the carnivorous limb.

Drasbart snatched the boatswain's fallen pistol axe from the deck and rushed to the man's aid. A single strike severed the frond through. He swung the weapon at the next two that were trying to attack him. Slicing through one, he dodged the other lunging for his weapon arm.

Geerhart grabbed a torch lying nearby and thrust the flame at the attacking tendril. Flaying madly from the pain, it retreated. Drasbart helped Geerhart to his feet, and they crossed to the few survivors huddled in a circle around the main mast. All had reverted to the torches, most of which showed signs of dying now the pitch-enthused wrappings at their tips had almost burned away.

When they had dragged the last of the casualties over the side, the rest of the stalks slithered back into the sea, giving the few weary survivors a welcome respite.

Drasbart's worried gaze traveled the length of the ship for any remaining threat. He was glad to see that, for now, the battle was over. A count of the remaining crew revealed no sign of Raf on the quarterdeck, another victim of the onslaught. They had taken a heavy toll. Only nine sailors, three of which were wounded, himself, the cabin boy and the captain, remained of those above deck. He wasn't sure how many wounded had made it below to visit the ship's surgeon to get patched up, but with the cook and the surgeon, he guessed maybe another three or four in total. In his estimate, the weed and creatures had claimed more than thirty souls since the ship had encountered them, and they still weren't free of the monsters' clutches. Their future looked grim. He looked around for the captain and spotted him reloading his pistol while crossing cautiously to the forecastle doorway. To find out what their next move would be, he went to intercept him.

Aiming his reloaded pistol through the doorway, Fokke peered into the gloomy stairwell.

"Anything wrong, Captain?"

Fokke glanced at him. "Plenty. That large creature's still on board."

Drasbart stared around the deck anxiously.

"It's not up here." Fokke nodded at the entrance. "It's down there."

With creased brow, Drasbart looked down the few wooden steps. "That's not good. There're men down there."

"No, it damn well isn't," stated Fokke irritably, brushing a hand through his blood-matted beard. He glanced over at the men gathered around the mast casting fearful gazes at the sides of the ship. "Gather half of the men able to wield a firearm and bring them to me."

"You're going down after it? Is that wise?"

Fokke nodded. "Perhaps not, but I mean to see it dead for what it's done here today. Even if I have to burn the ship around it to achieve that."

Unsure if the captain was serious, Drasbart nodded. "I'll go select the men."

"While we're below, you and the rest of the crew are to remain topside and guard the ship against further attack."

"I'm not sure that's even possible with the few we have left."

"You'll do your best, I'm sure. If we fail to return, load the landing boat with provisions, set a fire, and you and any others still alive abandon ship." He glanced at one of the landing boats, its canvas cover loosened by the strong winds draped over the side. "Best get Tom set bailing out the rainwater just in case."

"Aye." Hoping it wouldn't come to that, Drasbart went to issue the captain's orders to the few remaining members of the crew.

The ship's cook, Jon Busch, stopped gathering the pots, pans and other metal containers that would boil water and glanced along the corridor at the running footsteps approaching. Already nervous from the sounds of battle going on topside, which he noticed had now waned, he reached for the meat cleaver when the footsteps were almost upon him.

Wagner glanced at the cook as he sprinted by. "Hide, the devil's coming!"

Busch had peeked topside during the devilish weed's attack and had witnessed the crew fighting the carnivorous plant and evil creatures. He didn't for a moment doubt Wagner's warning and ducked behind the serving counter.

The patriarch jumped down the steps and stared along the corridor. Though the passage was dark, its nocturnal eyesight picked out every detail and the fleeing human at its end. Cautious of the strange, confining surroundings, it padded along the corridor at a swift gait. On reaching the galley, it paused and sniffed the strong stench of unwashed human.

Busch turned his frightened gaze to the end of the counter, and his ears to the deep, rumbling breaths of the devil creature Wagner had alerted him to. When its snout appeared past the edge, he raised the cleaver. He trembled when its head came into view and turned its horrendous face at him. As if sensing his presence, the tendrils on the creature's back pointed their tips in his direction and split open, revealing each had a small jaw lined with tiny, needle-sharp teeth.

The creature snarled and moved so swiftly, Busch barely registered the attack before it was upon him. Stumbling back as he swung the meat cleaver, stacks of pots and pans clattered to the floor. The knife joined them when a claw sliced at his wrist, cutting deep to the bone. Busch screamed. The creature bit down on his neck, severing arteries and windpipe and scraping teeth across his spine. Busch flopped to the floor when the monster released him. Its tongue slithered over its snout to lick off the cook's blood as it moved away to continue its hunt.

Wagner leaped down another set of steps as Busch's scream was cut short. Desperately gazing around the gundeck for a hiding place as the clack-clack of the creature's claws on the ship's timbers grew steadily closer, he rushed for the far door and pulled it shut it behind him. Breathing heavily from fear and exertion, he put an ear to the door. The ominous clacking continued to track him. He sniveled in terror as he grabbed one of the lanterns stored on hooks beside the entrance and lit it. Holding it high, he shone it around the storeroom filled with the heady aroma of spices. Stacked with crates, barrels, and sacks filled with expensive exotic wares and provisions for the long voyage home, it provided plenty of places to hide. Though doubtful any would prevent the monster from finding him, he nevertheless hung the lantern from a ceiling hook and sought one out.

On entering the gundeck, the creature paused and cast its evil gaze around in search of the human that had caused the painful throbbing wound in its side. It raised its head to the muffled screams, running footsteps and gunshots filtering down from the top deck, before focusing on the door at the far end of the room — the only route the human could have taken. It slowly crossed to it and putting its snout to the gap beneath the door, sniffed, drawing in the human's scent and fear. It slammed its shoulder into the barrier, sending it flying open to smash against the wall. It entered the storeroom, and sniffing the air tainted with strange aromas, it narrowed in on the human's scent and followed it through the room.

Shivering from the chilly, brackish water and fear of the thing that moved across the creaking boards above him, Wagner flinched when it smashed through the door. Backing deeper into the cold, dark keel hold he had chosen as his place of concealment; his eyes followed the creature's footsteps as its body blocked the lantern light seeping through gaps between the floorboards above. He sobbed when it halted at the trapdoor, its growl deep, rumbling and full of menace.

Wagner clamped a hand over his mouth to the stifle the involuntary fearful gasp brought forth when the creature flung the hatch open. Lowering his head and shoulders until his eyes were just above the surface of the foul soup, he stared at the monstrous demon poking its head through the opening. Its searching eyes turned in his direction. His whole body trembled when they found him, sending small ripples emanating out from his shaking form.

Wagner rose up straight when the creature dropped through the hatch and slipped beneath the surface. He sobbed as his terrified gaze fixated on the creature's tentacles, the only visible part of it, gliding closer, their tiny mouths chomping hungrily. He screamed when he was yanked under and swallowed the foul water tinged with his blood when the creature and its tentacles feasted.

CHAPTER 9

Defeated

Brackish water drained from the creature when it climbed out through the hatch and ran a black, pointed tongue over its teeth stained with the blood of its recent human meal. When distant voices promised another tasty feast, it skulked towards them.

Fighting the man's jerking movements with each prick of the needle he passed through his skin to knit the sides of the deep gash together, Tobias Smollett, the ship's surgeon, barber, and carpenter, continued with his task. Though he hadn't seen the creature responsible for the crew's recent injuries with his own eyes, the vivid descriptions given by his frightened patients had painted such a strange beast of immense ferociousness that he found it difficult to believe such a monster existed outside the realm of myth and nightmares. Something, though, had inflicted the severe wounds on those he had patched up, most of whom he doubted would survive the long journey home with what limited medical assistance he had at his disposal. He tied off the final stitch and cut the thread with his teeth.

After wiping his bloody hands on an already blood-soiled rag, Smollett reached for the man's mouth and removed the piece of teeth-dented wood his patient had bitten down on against the pain. "All done."

Grimacing from the fiery agony emanating from his wound, Jennet sat up on the makeshift wooden operating table that also served as a dining table for some of the men. He gratefully took the jug of medicinal rum the surgeon offered to bolster the pain-dulling rum he had supped before the doctor had patched him up.

Distracted by a soft clicking, the surgeon stepped outside the cordoned-off temporary operating room and gazed along the corridor. When he stared past the rows of hammocks strung across the forward sleeping quarters and along the gloomy corridor at the room's end, the clicks stopped. Spying nothing amiss and blaming his frayed nerves, he returned to the task of reorganizing his operating utensils for his next patient.

Cloaked in shadow, the patriarch halted when the human appeared and looked in its direction. Poised to attack if he approached, it relaxed when the human turned away. It bounded along the passage in swift, long leaps that carried it to the surgeon before Smollett had entirely shifted to investigate the sounds of its approach.

Smollett dropped the bone-saw he was about to re-sharpen and screamed from shock and fear at the creature leaping at him.

The creature crashed into Smollett, slamming him into the small instrument table, spilling bloodstained metal instruments to the floor. Its teeth savaged the man's chest, biting through skin and bone and tearing away a large chunk of flesh and broken ribs. As the corpse slid to the floor, the creature turned its head to the other human in the room.

Smollett's last thought before he died was that the descriptions his patients had told of the creature were indeed founded in fact and hadn't done it justice.

With the rum paused at his lips, Jennet stared at the monster chewing flesh and crunching bone, Smollett's blood dripping from its jaws. Since it seemed content to finish its gruesome morsel before attacking, Jennet threw the jug at it and dived for the canvas wall which divided the operating room from the rest of the sleeping quarters. He stumbled, ripping the canvas sheet from its moorings when he tripped to the floor. With it still wrapped partly around him, he crawled for the exit.

While still ingesting its recent meal, the creature padded over to the crawling human and pinned the canvas sheet to the floor with a claw.

Tugging on the entwined canvas impeding his progress, Jennet rolled onto his back to free himself of the obstruction. He trembled at seeing the monster up so close and whimpered when it moved closer and stopped astride him. When the creature lowered its head to his face and ran its tongue along his cheek, Jennet passed out with shock. The creature nudged the human's head with his snout, but when his eyes failed to open, he dragged an eyelid up with a claw and stared into the man's rolled-back eye. A snore swept the creature's gaze to another human asleep in a hammock strung from the ceiling. Its savage gaze around the room picked out four men, oblivious to what was going around them in their rum-sedated unconsciousness.

It picked up Jennet and tossed him onto its back. Its tentacles held him in place as it crossed to Smollett's corpse, gripped his head in its jaws and dragging him beneath its body, headed back along the corridor. After dumping the meals in the keel hold to prevent the weeds their kind had allied with from taking them, the creature returned to the crew's sleeping quarters for more to add to its pantry.

◆

Accompanied by the creaking of the gently rolling vessel, Fokke led the four frightened men along the corridor, searching each dark nook, chamber and possible hiding place large enough to conceal the monster. They discovered the first sign of the monster's trail in the galley.

Eneass Orich stared at the puddle of blood leaking from the cook's corpse behind the counter. His anxious gaze followed the blood trail left by the creature's paws that led deeper into the ship.

Fokke glanced around at the frightened men and tried to offer them some encouragement, whether he believed it or not. "Down here it can only come at us from one direction. Stay alert, together, and we'll see an end to this."

He led them forward.

Shocked awake by the freezing water, Jennet opened his eyes. Choking on the foul water pouring into his mouth, he thrashed to the surface. Unable to believe he was still alive and, based on the lack of any new pain, uninjured by the monster, he looked around his dark surroundings. Slivers of light shone through gaps in the floorboards above him and the open hatch at the far end. Smollett's corpse bobbed in the water a short distance away. Though he had no idea how he had come to be here, he waded over to the open hatch.

Jennet was about to haul himself through the opening when approaching clacks of claws froze him. Assuming it must be the large creature he had encountered earlier, he lowered himself down gently and glanced around the keel hold for a hiding place. There was none. He waded over to Smollett's floating corpse, dragged it to the far end of the chamber, and turned it sideways. Holding it to prevent it from drifting away, Jennet tilted back, so his face was above water but hidden by the corpse. Trying his utmost not to panic, he listened to the monster's heavy footsteps crossing to the hatch. He almost whimpered when something splashed into the water. The resulting ripples swayed the corpse and washed water over his face. A second splash followed. The footfalls moved away.

Almost sobbing in relief, Jennet stood up. When the creature's footsteps had faded into silence, he crossed to the hatch. Nudging aside the two fresh corpses, he climbed out.

With silent haste, he crossed the hold and checked the gundeck was safe before entering. Aware the creature was probably above him somewhere, he headed for one of the cannons and opened the gun port. It would be a tight squeeze, but it was a discomfort he'd gladly bear to avoid running into the creature again. Headfirst, he squirmed through the opening, scraping the skin from his shoulders when he forced them through. Casting an anxious gaze at the kelp below that hadn't sensed his presence yet, he halted on hearing the telltale clacks of the creature's claws approaching. Increasing his speed, he squeezed through the tight passage and hanging from the side of the ship; he quietly closed the gun port.

The patriarch entered the gundeck dragging a body and passed through without glancing at the gun port where Jennet perched outside.

When he was sure the creature had gone, Jennet climbed the hull. He poked his head above the rail and screamed when agonizing flames were thrust at his face, blistering his skin, scalding his eyes and setting his hair on fire. He toppled back and fell into the welcoming embrace of the kelp stalks that quickly whisked him away.

All heads on deck turned to the scream and focused on Klaas van Twillert standing by the rail, his expression mortified.

"It was Jennet," Klaas explained, his voice shaky. "I thought it was one of those things and panicked."

Aware that it was too late to help Jennet now that the weed had him, the men returned to their duties and focused on their survival.

An agonized scream rang out from below. Three shots followed in quick succession. Another piercing cry. An angry curse from the captain. A shriek from the creature. Silence.

Drasbart rushed to the forecastle entrance and gazed worriedly down the steps; his ear cocked for sounds of life his low expectations held no hope of hearing. After a few moments of indecisive apprehension, he descended to the lower deck and peered along the corridor. Soft growls and grunts drifted up from the ship's bowels and grew steadily louder, closer. In the far reaches of the gloom, something dark and menacing appeared and directed its evil gaze upon him. When it bounded towards him with a bone-chilling shriek, Drasbart fled up the stairs, slammed the door shut and secured it with the storm lock. He hoped the creature wasn't intelligent enough to figure out how to unlock it from the other side. He stepped back when the beast thudded against it. Praying it would hold, he stared at the door shuddering from a second blow.

Hell Ship

When the creature's claw-clicks moved away, he turned his gaze along the deck and on the men focused on the rails. "Oric! Batten the aft door, now!"

Sensing the urgency in the first mate's order, Oric shoved the pistol in his waistband and rushed to the stern. He released the door catch holding it open as thumps from below grew closer far too swiftly. As he swung the door closed, he glimpsed the creature appearing at the bottom of the steps. He slammed the door against the frame. His hand gripped the storm lock. The door crashed open with a splintering of cracked timber, which sent Oric was sprawling. The creature landed beside him and swept its malicious gaze around the deck before staring at its fallen victim. Oric reached for the pistol stuck in his waistband. A claw on his arm halted the move. He sobbed when the creature's head filled his vision. He screamed when its teeth ripped his flesh.

When the creature appeared on deck, Drasbart saw the tired and bedraggled group of six men—the last surviving members of the crew that had set out on this fateful journey—cautiously approach the creature. Drasbart lit his torch from the nearest lantern and holding the blunderbuss ready to fire, joined the men converging on the beast.

Releasing its jaws from Oric's body, which trembled for a few moments before he died, the creature glanced at the approaching humans. Aware the weapons they wielded would cause it pain, it raised its head and let out a long shriek before leaping up to the poop deck.

Drasbart and the crew directed frightened glances at the rails when a cacophony of shrieks, squeals, and claws climbing the hull came from both sides of the ship. A dark slick, formed of the smaller monstrosities, poured onto the deck. The men backed away and formed a defensive circle. Their torches and firearms swept over the approaching hoard promising death and pain that they all knew couldn't be held at bay for long.

A blunderbuss aimed at the hoard's front edge blasted powerful, deadly shot at the creatures, although they all knew that the few it killed would fail to make any significant impact on their numbers.

Recognizing the uselessness of the situation, one man put his pistol barrel in his mouth, pulled the trigger, and flopped on the deck. More shots killed and maimed a few of the beasts. The men threw their discharged weapons at the creatures which clattered as they hit the wooden boards. Torches jabbed and swung at the demon creatures, but there were too many to hold back. They overwhelmed the men, and their agony and screams soon faded into silence.

Having observed the slaughter of the last humans aboard from the poop deck, the patriarch placed its front limbs on the rail, raised its head and let out a triumphant wailing screech.

CHAPTER 10

Pirates

Concealed in the small landing boat used to convey officers to other ships at sea, crew to shore to restock provisions, or to rescue a man overboard if sea and weather conditions were favorable, Tom had paused his bailing out of the rainwater and watched in horror the slaughter of the last of his crewmates. He ducked lower behind the gunwale when the giant monster padded down the quarterdeck steps. Its smaller brethren dodged its aggressive tentacles when they snapped at any too close. It halted by Dragbert's corpse which the smaller creatures had been feasting on, picked it up in its jaws, and dragged it below deck.

Trembling with fear that the creatures would discover and devour him, Tom pulled a canvas sheet over him and prayed they would soon leave. His only chance of survival was to wait until they had gone, launch the boat and flee the hell ship. As the day wore on, fatigued from recent events and lack of rest, Tom was unable to keep his eyes open and drifted off to sleep.

Awoken by a jolt and bleary-eyed from a fitful sleep filled with nightmare creatures, Tom listened to the pattering of rain on the canvas covering him. Worried another storm was about to hit, he pulled the sheet back and froze at the sight of the Jolly Rodger flag fluttering in the stiff breeze at the top of a mast from the ship pulled alongside the Fortuyn. *Pirates.*

Keeping low, he cautiously peered over the side of the small boat. Pirates armed with various firearms, cutlasses and other sharp-bladed weapons, furtively moved across the deck. Their murderous faces turned this way and that, searching for the crew of the vessel they planned to plunder.

One of the pirates halted at the fired weapons and burnt-out torches scattered around the area where the last of the crew had staged their final battle. He picked up a pistol and studied it for a moment before slipping it in his belt. Noticing the blood, some strangely dark, mingling with rain lashing the deck, he turned his head and whistled low and shrill.

Pirate Captain Thomas Trent, referred to by King William III as a *"wicked and ill-disposed person,"* glanced at the man who had attracted his attention and walked over. "What is it, Skank?"

Skank pointed his pistol at the deck. "Blood, Captain."

Trent swept his cruel gaze over the rain-diluted blood splashes dotted around the deck. From the amount spilled blood, burnt-out torches—an oddity aboard a wooden vessel—and discarded weapons, it was apparent that there had been a brutal battle fought here. Pondering the whereabouts of the victors and why they hadn't claimed the weapons, his eyes shifted to gaze the length of the ship.

"Maybe other pirates have beaten us to the prize," suggested Skank.

Trent shook his head. "We're the only ones foolish enough to be out in this weather."

They had been returning from yet another unsuccessful attack on a ship they suspected was loaded with valuable spices and cargo. It had proved too heavily gunned for them to take. They had been lucky to escape with as little damage to their ship as they had received. It had been their second failure in as many weeks, and the murmurs amongst the crew didn't bode well for Trent's prolonged captaincy.

Their bad luck had continued when they ran into a violent storm that saw two men tossed overboard into the merciless sea. Keen to boost his disgruntled crew's morale and his reputation, he had given the order to attack when they spotted the lightly armed Dutch ship. Though they had the cannons at the ready, and the topside crew was prepared for a fight, not a shot had been fired. They had come alongside, grappled her, and still, there was no appearance of the crew.

Trent glanced up at the angry dark clouds as the increasing strength of the waves crashed the two ships together. Maybe it hadn't been such a good idea to come here to plunder ships freshly stocked with valuable cargo. He had hoped to get them before they reached the seas infested with his fellow pirates all eager to claim the richest prizes. The non-appearance of anyone aboard, whether original crew or the interlopers responsible for the bloodshed worried Trent. It could be a trap set to be sprung when they ventured below. If that were the case, they wouldn't catch him.

Trent turned to Skank. "Send half the men below to see what cargo she carries and inform them to be wary of anyone who might wait in ambush. But be quick about it. If the storm gets any rougher, we'll have to cut the Fortuyn free or risk damaging my ship."

"Aye, Captain." Skank rushed off to carry out his orders.

From his place of concealment, Tom observed the group of pirates split off from the others and move to bow and stern.

With weapons ready to slaughter anyone they came across, they headed below deck. The remaining pirates guarded the topside with their captain; their gazes focused on the two entrances ready to dispatch anyone not of their crew if they appeared.

Worried about the threat from the pirates and the creatures that might still be nearby, Tom decided to remain hidden. He could see no sign of the monstrous fiends, so if they had gone, maybe the pirates would plunder the ship's cargo and leave too so he could carry out his original plan of escaping in the small boat. If the pirates commandeered the Fortuyn, he would have no choice but to reveal himself and pray for their mercy.

Pistol shots followed screams from below and caused those on deck to aim their weapons and anxious gazes at the two aft and bow below deck entrances.

Trent strode to the bow door and aimed one of his pistols below at the sound of footsteps rushing for the exit. One of his men appeared and screamed as he fell to the floor, smashing his face on the boards with a hard thud that broke cartilage. Before he could stand, he was yanked back out of sight. The screams of his men that had ventured below fell to silence.

Believing the Fortuyn's crew had sprung their trap, the captain whistled the signal for his remaining men to attack. Yelling battle cries, the pirates headed below.

Oblivious to the threat boarding their ship, the Amity, the few pirates that had remained onboard stared across at the Fortuyn. Confident their comrades would soon dispatch those who had attacked; they waited for it to be over. Then they would discover what valuable cargo the ship carried. All would receive a fair share of the prize money when they sold the booty.

The creatures that had swum around the pirate ship climbed up the port hull and over the rail. Splitting off into groups, each selected a victim and attacked.

The captain turned his gaze away from the second series of screams coming from below and stared across at the commotion coming from the *Amity*. He stared in disbelief at the variety of different sized creatures attacking his men. They swarmed over them, stabbing claws and ripping teeth into flesh. The crew didn't stand a chance. One man fled up the rigging. A few creatures set off in pursuit and caught him before he reached the first yardarm. Screaming and pulling at the animals on his body, he fell to the deck. His neck broke with a ghastly crack when his head took the full brunt of his plummet.

Trent turned back to the doorway when clacks on the boards announced something wicked approached. He backed away when more of the evil creatures appeared and raced up the steps. With his escape route now blocked, Trent fired his two pistols, which he then discarded as there was no time to reload, drew his cutlass and raced for the side of the ship. He leaped across to the Amity, slicing at any creatures in his path. When his anxious gaze around the deck revealed most of his crew on board were either dead, dying, or still fighting the beasts, he fled to his cabin. The creatures that spotted him followed.

Fighting through the few creatures that had ventured below, Trent entered his cabin and slammed the door shut. He turned the key in the lock and stepped back when the pursuing creatures thudded against it. Hoping it would withstand the barrage, he focused on the door. Panting heavily from terror and his run, he sunk into his padded chair when they changed tactics and started scratching their sharp claws on it. He cocked an ear to the door when the screeches and scratching suddenly ceased. *Had they given up and gone in search of easier prey?*

A series of heavier clacking claw-steps grew louder as they approached. Something bigger had arrived. Trent pictured one of the smaller creatures larger; it would be formidable, vicious and inescapable. He trembled at the thought of his impending, painful death. The ominous clacks halted outside the door. Something growled, deep and menacing, heightening his fear, something he hadn't experienced for a long time. He had faced overwhelming odds in battles during his pirate profession, but that was against men, not this hoard of hell-spawned devils.

Trent pushed back into his chair and cursed his quaking legs. He grabbed a bottle of rum from a desk drawer and gulped down a long swig to top up his waning courage. Startled when a claw struck the door with enough force to penetrate through with a splintering crack of timber, he watched the large hooked talon rip at the wood when it withdrew. Two more wood splintering blows created a gap large enough for the creature responsible to look through. Quaking with terror, Trent stared into its bright, evil eyes.

When it snarled at him and attacked the door with increased ferocity, Trent grabbed the lantern from a ceiling hook and threw it at the door. The lamp smashed, sending burning oil spraying through the gap. The splintered door whooshed into flame, causing the creature to screech and cease its attack. Driven back by the heat, it peered through the fire at him. Trent threw the rum at it, adding more fuel to the fire. Unable to reach its prey blocked by the flames, the large creature raced away with its smaller brethren following.

With his courage infused by his small victory, the will to survive surged through Trent. He moved to a large chest, opened it and stared at the precious plunder within; it was too vast for him to be able to save it all. The crackle of flames creeping into the room spurred him into action. He fished a silver chest the length of his forearm from the booty, and regretting the loss of the stolen treasure; he rushed to the window. He flung it open and as he climbed out noticed the strange seaweed gathering around the hull. Another oddity to add to today's strange events. He scaled the stern and peered over the rail.

As he gazed across the flame-and smoke-washed deck at his dead crew being feasted on by their vicious killers, a shadow moving across the rail he clung to alerted him to danger much closer. He swung his cutlass when he twisted to confront it and sliced through three stalks. As they wavered frantically spewing their dark sap-blood, Trent glimpsed movement by the midship rail. It wasn't anyone from his crew. Surprised someone had survived the creature's wrath, he climbed over the railing and concealed himself behind the wheel, watching to see what the person would do.

Fearful he would be spotted by the creatures when they appeared, Tom had remained flat in the boat as he listened to their piercing yells and the screams of the pirate crew as they had slaughtered them. When all sounds of battle had ceased for a few moments, he risked a peek over the gunwale.

Hell Ship

Except for a few creatures milling around the deck, the Fortuyn seemed deserted. He turned his gaze to the pirate ship. Groups of animals were feasting on their slaughtered victims while another group gathered around the stern doorway. They suddenly moved away when smoke poured over them from below. The ship was aflame. The giant creature leaped through the smoke and shrilled to the others before returning to the Fortuyn. The smaller animals followed his lead and abandoned the pirate ship. Some dived into the sea; others jumped across to the Fortuyn.

Unaware the flames would consume both vessels if left tethered, some of the creatures followed the big one below Fortuyn's deck. Though some lingered topside to lick up spilled blood and fight over scraps of flesh, the majority of those remaining climbed over the side and returned to the weed.

Tom stared at the smoke pouring from the bow doorway and turned his attention back to the Fortuyn and the few creatures moving about.

Realizing he needed to make a decision, and quickly, Tom believed he stood a better chance of surviving on the burning pirate ship than the monster-infested Fortuyn. Praying the creatures wouldn't spot him, he climbed the winch line fixed to the small boat's bow and swung onto the rigging, before climbing up to the lower yardarm, running along its length and leaping across. He grabbed the rigging aboard the pirate ship and dropped to the deck. Keeping low, he moved to the starboard side and gazed back at the Fortuyn. One of the creatures perched on the sterncastle glanced in his direction briefly before turning back to devouring the morsel of flesh it had snatched from its brethren. Keen to be free of the savage fiends and turn his thoughts to his escape from the burning vessel, Tom turned away and moved along the rail to the nearest grappling rope holding the two ships together. Using his knife, he sawed through until it snapped free.

A creature turned its head to the sound of a grappling hook clattering to the Fortuyn's deck. Spying no threat and nothing it could eat, it turned away and continued lapping up the blood from the deck boards.

After observing the boy the pirate captain assumed had come from the Fortuyn begin severing the grappling ropes, Trent crept from his hiding place and climbed down the quarterdeck steps.

Tom moved along the starboard side cutting through the ropes, and the two ships drifted apart a little more. When there was only the tether nearest the bow remaining, the pirate ship's stern swung out. The bow scraped along the Fortuyn's and swiveled on its off-center restraint. Wood splintered when the two ship's ground against each other. The bowsprit snapped when it snagged on the Fortuyn's rigging, and the mermaid figurehead on the prow was ripped off.

"What's yer plan, boy?"

Tom almost stumbled to the deck when he spun to face the voice, his knife poised to attack.

"You'll need a bigger weapon than that toothpick to take me down, boy," said Trent, grinning.

Tom lowered the small weapon and glanced briefly at the small silver chest tucked under the pirate captain's arm. "Cut the ships free and then use one of the landing boats to escape your burning ship."

Trent nodded his agreement. "Aye, lad. A sound plan. But before we do, best we grab some victuals to sustain us as we're a long way from land."

He glanced at the smoke and flames pouring from the stern doorway and then at the forward door. The wind sweeping below funneled the smoke toward the stern, leaving the bow entrance relatively smoke-free. He refocused on the boy.

"I'll cut the final line, grab us a cask of water and prepare the boat for launching while you nip to the galley and grab us some provisions. Cook was preparing a meal when we spotted your ship, so if those monsters haven't gobbled it up, there should be some cooked meat down there."

Though unsure he could trust the pirate, Tom was low on options. "Aye, Captain." Fighting the rolling of the ship, he sprinted for the entrance to the bow, and after checking it was free of flame, and creatures, headed below.

The creature on the aft deck that had been observing the two humans leaped down, jumped onto the starboard rail and scampered along it. When another noticed its brethren's sudden activity, it gazed across at the other ship to work out its objective.

Spying the human meal its excited brethren headed for, it rushed to the rail to try and be the first to reach it.

A swift strike from Trent's cutlass severed the last rope holding the two ships together. Gradually the wind and waves moved them apart. A movement cast his gaze to the side. His cutlass swung at the creature leaping across the gap between the two ships and sliced it in two. Both halves landed on the deck and continued moving. The front half dragged its amputated body toward the captain's foot. A swift stamp of his boot crushed it to a pulpy mess. Trent gasped and staggered back when a slightly larger version of the creature slammed into his chest and clawed at his skin. The silver casket slipped from his grasp and sprung open when it struck the deck, spraying diamonds, rubies and other precious gems in all directions. Trent frantically slammed the cutlass pommel into the creature while trying to pull it free with his other hand. Ripping off a clawed limb, he threw it to the deck and grabbed another. The creature snapped at his fingers, biting a tip clean off. Stepping back, Trent slipped on the jewels and fell, smashing the back of his head against the boards. The creature continued its attack and furiously sliced talons across his chest and neck, shredding the captain's throat. As the pirate's life faded, the beast feasted.

Flames devoured anything that would burn as the fire crept hungrily through the wooden ship — turning goods, furniture, walls, and doors to charred devastation. Finding its way to the gunpowder store, it lapped at the stacked barrels of black powder.

Tom was thrown to the floor by the force of the explosion. Ripped apart timber and deadly splinters filled the air, killing any monsters within the blast radius. After the rocking subsided, the ship remained at a list. Water gurgled into the splintered hole blasted below the waterline. The vessel was now not only aflame but also sinking.

Tom climbed to his feet. Using the walls to steady himself against the incline and the rolling of the pitching ship, he entered the galley. A sound froze him to the spot. His frightened gaze focused on the end of the serving counter from where the slurping, grunting noises came. Aware it was imperative he salvaged as many provisions as possible before the sea claimed the vessel and him, Tom forced his legs into motion. Cautiously edging left, his feet picked a silent route through the pots, pans and kitchen utensils scattered across the floor. He peered at the head and chest of the corpse poking past the counter's end, its face frozen in terrified, agonized death. Tom assumed it was the pirate cook the captain had mentioned. The head lolled to the side. Its lifeless fear-frozen gaze stared into Tom's, which was just as scared. The head of a small creature appeared, paler than the others he had seen, a creamy gray with what looked like pink blisters on its body. It crawled up the cook's torn-open corpse and began feasting on his face. Latching teeth on a lip, it pulled until a chunk was torn free.

After devouring the morsel, it moved in for more but stopped, sniffed the air and turned its evil head to Tom's position.

As its head turned, Tom ducked down behind the end of the counter. He thought the creature he hadn't seen him, but after a few moments, he heard its slow approach.

Water flowed into the galley as the ship dipped its stern, reminding Tom that it was slowly sinking, and his time aboard was fast running out. The creature's movements had ceased. *Had it gone? Had it returned to feasting on the cook?*

The ship jolted to the side when the seawater that was filling its bowels adjusted to a new level from its shifting weight. Tom needed to move before the vessel became his coffin and the seabed his grave. He climbed to his feet and came face-to-face with the creature perched on the serving counter. The beast snarled as it hunched, ready to spring. Fighting the lopsided and tipping angle of the ship, Tom grabbed a hanging pot from its hook and slammed it down on the abomination's head. Dark goo splattered the counter. He cautiously lifted it. The dark glutinous blood stretched like melted cheese between counter and pot base. He dodged back with a gasp when small versions of the creature scurried from blisters splitting open on its abdomen like spiders hatching from their eggs. He whacked them with the pot and moved away.

His quick gaze around the kitchen spied a pan on the stove tipped on its side. He crossed to it and pulled the hunk of meat from amongst the steaming heap of stewed vegetables; it was the pirates' meal the cook had been preparing when he and those who would have eaten it became a meal themselves. He grabbed a sack that still had a few potatoes in it, added the gravy-dripping joint and scooped inside some raw vegetables littering the preparation area. A glance back at the counter revealed the tiny devils that had survived the battering crawling across it. Slinging the heavy sack over a shoulder, he sloshed through the water. Battling the increasingly acute angles of the ship, Tom struggled along the corridor and climbed the steps.

His gaze around the deck picked out the lifeless form of the captain being hoisted into the air by weed tendrils which dragged him over the side. His eyes spotted things sparkling on the deck and the sliding silver chest they had spilled from, which had come to a halt against a cannon. Though he had never owned or held any precious stones, they were easily recognizable for what they were. With his wary gaze on the stalks slithering back over the side, Tom placed his ration sack against the foremast and cautiously moved to the captain's dropped cutlass lying in a pool of his blood. He snatched it up, crossed to the chest and fell to a knee beside it. Tom righted the chest and scooped handfuls of the precious gems into it. Noticing the small arm of one of the crab creatures, he added it to the chest. Proof the unbelievable story he would tell of what happened aboard the Fortuyn was true.

Shadows of tentacles on the boards turned him around. He swung the sword at the two menacing stalks and sliced through them both. As they wavered frantically spewing their dark sap-blood, Tom closed the lid, tucked the chest under his arm and backed away.

After retrieving the sack, Tom headed for the nearest of the three landing boats lashed to the deck. The route was made more hazardous by the objects sliding and rolling across it from the ship's steadily increasing tipping, and rolling movements as it was slowly dragged under by the waves. He grabbed the side of the boat to steady himself and dropped the sack and chest inside. He briefly thought of going to collect one of the smaller water barrels the captain had failed to procure, essential for his survival, but the imminent sinking of the ship cautioned him against it until he had the boat ready to launch for a quick getaway.

Tom climbed in the boat and slashed the ties with his knife. As he freed it from its tethers, it slid down the sloping deck and crashed into the side of the sterncastle. Peering through the doorway at the seawater almost filling the stairwell and focusing on the two dots of light below the surface growing closer, raising his cutlass when the creature broke the surface. Thrown off balance when the ship rolled sharply, he stumbled and fell on his back. The cutlass slipped from his hand and clattered to the deck. The creature jumped onto the bow, screeched its battle cry and bared its teeth at him. Tom grabbed his knife and sliced through the thin rope securing the oars to the seats. With no time to stand, he grabbed one and swung it at the creature when it leaped at him. The blow cracked limbs and sent the creature flying. Tom gripped the side of the boat, pulled himself up and searched for the creature. He spied it a short distance away. Even though it had two broken limbs, and its hard carcass cracked, leaking dark blood, it still dragged itself across the sloping deck, its murderous eyes focused on its aggressor.

A group of three small water barrels straining against their moorings broke free and tumbled down the deck. One rolled to the side and came to a halt against the rail, another struck the rear of Tom's boat, hurtled away and tossed overboard, the third rolled over the creature, squashing it into a dark stain on the deck, clipped the rear of a cannon and bounced into the air. Tom ducked to avoid the barrel aiming directly for him. It skimmed over his head, struck the sterncastle wall and dropped into the boat. Unable to believe his luck — the water would last for weeks — Tom swiftly fastened the life-sustaining cask to the seat. He gripped the sides when the boat slid and skewed to the side with the cumulative tilting of the ship. It wouldn't be long now before the pirate vessel slipped beneath the waves. The bow of the small boat jolted against the rail, rode up over it and dropped into the sea with a jolting splash that threw Tom from his seat.

Hauling his battered body upright, Tom sat and looked behind at the ship's bow rising gracefully skywards. With flames creeping up its decks and smoke and steam from sea-extinguished fires pouring from the broken shell, for a few moments it hung there as if undecided what to do next. Slowly, with a straining creak of timbers and cracking and splintering of wood, the flaming hulk tipped to the side.

Tom grabbed two oars and frantically rowed his small vessel out of the path of the sinking ship before it rolled on top of him. The main mast, still hung with sails flapping from sagging lines ready to tighten for the pirates' getaway, splashed into the sea beside his boat. Rocked by the resulting surge, Tom glanced around at the objects bobbing to the surface as the sea swept through the submerged parts of the ship it was never meant to enter, flushing out anything buoyant not lashed down.

Keen to salvage what he could, Tom cut the trim sail free from the wood and collected some lengths of rope. After hauling everything into the boat, he glanced at the masts dipping beneath the surface. The ship was rolling bottom up. Aware his rowing strength would soon desert him, he filled his lungs and dived into the sea. He swam to the topmost yardarm and wrapped his legs around it. Carried deeper by the submerging ship, he sliced at the trailing lines securing the top yardarm in place, shimmied along it and unscrewed the pin from the jointing shackle fixed to the mast. The ship dragged him deeper and deeper, but he was unwilling to give up until his lungs threatened to burst. Objects sunk past him, ropes trailed in the currents like the arms of an octopus reaching for him. As soon as the pin was free, he unlinked the yardarm and pushed it away. As he swam and directed the timber spar away from the sinking vessel, Tom stared in amazement at the sight of the upside-down ship slipping past him on its journey to the seabed incalculable fathoms below.

Hell Ship

With lungs burning, Tom swam for the surface and gulped down air as soon as his head emerged free of the water. He turned until he spied his drifting boat and swam over to the yardarm. Placing his hands on it, and kicking it with his feet until it banged against the side. He climbed aboard and heaved the yardarm onboard.

Though he wanted to rest his tired and bruised body, Tom knew he only had one chance to salvage anything of use from amongst the floating debris before it sunk or drifted too far away to reach. The Fortuyn, under the control of no one but the weed and the creatures, drifted with the current a hundred yards distant. Whatever direction he headed, he wouldn't be going that way. He grabbed the oars and rowed through the debris, salvaging anything he thought might prove useful on his shipwrecked journey to land.

Over the coming days, he rigged a surprisingly effective sail with the yardarm. Using the rising sun as a reference, he navigated southeast in the hope of running across another ship sailing the lucrative trade route or, preferably, reaching the African coast and following it to the nearest port.

During his lonesome journey, he had plenty of time to ponder the terrible events aboard the Fortuyn and the demise of the pirates. Even with the creature's limb proving the strange sea beasts existed, the tale was so incredible people would think him insane when he told them about the carnivorous seaweed and sea monsters that had slaughtered his crewmates and officers and sailed away with the Fortuyn. He had trouble believing it himself, and he had witnessed it. He gazed behind anxiously as he had done a thousand times since heading away from the accursed ship he feared would pursue him. Tom believed it was doubtful the Fortuyn would remain afloat for long, unmanned, in the turbulent weather of the region. He decided it would be best if he blamed the loss of life, and the ship, on a sudden violent storm. The storm had claimed the lives of all except him, who was lucky enough to climb aboard the landing boat set adrift when the Fortuyn slipped beneath the waves. It was a story all would sympathize with and readily believe. As to the truth, that he would keep to himself.

On his sixth day at sea, Tom sighted the African coast and sailed along it until he approached the port of Cape Town. It had been founded by the Dutch East India Company to supply their passing ships with fresh fruits, vegetables, and meat, as well as to enable sailors wearied by the sea to recuperate. There were better locations along this Table Bay stretch of coast to construct a port, but none that had the supply of fresh water found here.

When he glimpsed Cape Town in the distance, Tom navigated through the rocks littering the surf and landed in a secluded cove. He collected his sack containing the chest of jewels, gave the boat a nod of thanks for bringing him safely to shore and headed for Cape Town. On his arrival, he became just another faceless stranger among the many sailors, merchantmen, and tradesmen passing through the town.

CHAPTER 11

Slave Ship Hannibal

After trading a few small rubies for some cash-the greedy merchantman receiving the better end of the deal-Tom set off to find a tavern where he could get a meal. With his hunger and thirst sated, he brought some new clothes. Though keen to return to his home in England, Tom couldn't yet face setting to sea again with the nightmarish events so fresh in his mind. He sought out lodgings and booked a room for the duration of his stay, however long that proved to be.

Over the coming weeks, visiting sailors told of a ghost ship sailing the seas around the African coast that was sometimes seen flying above the waves. Due to the recent disappearance of the

Fortuyn, its Dutch captain and crew, the spectral ship soon became known as the Flying Dutchman.

When Tom decided he had spent long enough in Cape Town, he pushed aside his fears and visited the busy port. It was a further month before he was able to book passage aboard a suitable ship to convey him back to England. A Dutch-owned wooden-hulled 700-ton East Indiaman, the *Eendracht,* captained by Dirk Hartog. The *Eendracht* was on its way home to Holland from a scientific expedition to Australia and would set sail in three days after restocking provisions. Tom would then purchase passage on a ship from Holland back to England.

Glancing up from his meal at the tavern where he ate almost daily, Tom observed the man, a sailor by his garb, who entered and rushed to the bar.

"Rum!" the man demanded.

The barkeeper eyed the scruffy-clothed seaman. "Let's see yer means to pay first." He had been duped too many times to get caught out again.

The haggard sailor duly complied and dumped a handful of coins on the counter. "Leave the bottle."

The barkeeper placed the rum bottle and a jug in front of the man and counted out the cost from the coins.

"Yer seems a little worse fer wear," commented a man taking a seat beside the sailor and eyeing the rum bottle longingly.

The free drink he hoped for wasn't forthcoming.

Noticing the man's covetous gaze upon his bottle, the sailor pulled it nearer to him. "So would yer if yer'd seen what these eyes of mine have been forced ter bear witness to."

Still hopeful of receiving a free tickle of rum, the man placed his empty tankard on the bar in plain view of his newfound companion. "And what was it yer witnessed that's shaken yer so?"

The sailor stared at the man. "Sea monsters! Evil fiends from the deep that killed most of me fellow crewmen; that's what."

Tom's ears pricked up at the mention of sea monsters.

"Sea monsters, was it?" commented the man in a disbelieving tone. Sailors were always talking about the weird sights they'd allegedly seen at sea. *Rum visions*, he called them.

"It was," stated the sailor. "Devils from below Davy Jones would be afeared of." He took another healthy swig of rum.

Realizing he wasn't going to get a single tot, and unwilling to listen to yet another delusory tale from an overly superstitious sailor, the thirsty man sighed, picked up his empty tankard and moved away.

"Yer don't look like yer've had a decent meal in recent memory."

The sailor turned his head and sized up Tom. "What's it ter yer, boy?"

"If yer'd be willing, I'd like to bear witness to yer tale," replied Tom. "There'll be a hot meal and another bottle of rum in it fer yer if yer oblige."

The seaman pondered the offer. His belly had been absent a hot meal far too long, and rum was always welcome. "Okay, sonny, I'll partake of some victuals wiv yer."

"And yer'll tell me yer story?"

The man nodded.

Tom attracted the barkeeper's attention. "Bring 'im what I've just had."

Tom put the payment in the barkeep's outstretched hand and turned to the sailor. "Let's go ter my table over there."

The sailor glanced at the table indicated by the boy and taking his drink with him followed him to the far corner of the room.

Observing the man's anxious disposition, one he'd worn not too long ago, Tom watched the man refill his tankard and sup it down in one. "Why don't yer begin while we're waiting fer yer victuals ter arrive?"

Though hesitant to relive the nightmare, he had struck a deal, and he intended to uphold his end of the bargain. "I was crewing aboard the slave ship, Hannibal, bound for the Americas with a hold crammed with Negros, when five days ago we encountered the wreckage of a vessel…

⇢◇⇠

The fifty-three slaves that included men, women, and five children, stowed on the upper slave deck—another equally packed with the abducted lay below them—awoke from their fitful sleep when something struck the wooden hull with a loud resonating boom. Aware they were below water level, and any damage to the old ship's hull could cause water to pour in, drowning them all, their anxious eyes followed the unseen object scraping and banging along the hull. Whatever their worth to the white men who had taken them from their homes, families, and lands, it would be doubtful any would risk their lives saving them.

Two more objects rebounded and banged along the other side of the hull.

They turned their worried gazes aloft and listened to the voices on deck.

"Debris ahead, turn port fifteen degrees," shouted one of the crew.

"Aye, sir. Turning fifteen degrees to port."

"What's happening, Martaigo?" asked Ghar, one of the captured men, his tone hushed and anxious.

Martaigo shrugged. "Like us all, this is my first time on such a vessel, and I don't understand their talk, but likely we've run into some wreckage."

"Does that mean we've reached land?" asked Sowar a short distance away in the darkness, her arm wrapped around a small frightened girl she had taken under her care.

"I can't see through wood, so I'm as wise as you all, but I doubt it. We've only been a few moons from our homes," answered Martaigo. "Let's wait to see what happens. But now we're from our slumber, return to trying to free yer chains, but quietly. If they suspect our doings, brutally punished or killed, we'll be."

"I fail to understand these white men," commented Jarvay. "They travel across the seas in large boats and steal us from our families, friends, and villages, and then commit us ter the harshest conditions imaginable." He tapped the ceiling brushing the top of his head in his hunched-over sitting position, "What little food they give us is almost inedible, barely enough water to keep us alive, and constantly beat us fer no reason. Why?"

Martaigo turned to the man who had spoken. "I would concentrate your thoughts and energy on freeing your manacles and not try fathoming the unfathomable ways of the cruel white skins. Nothing they've done so far makes me believe our lives will undergo any improvement when we arrive at our destination. Getting free, overtaking the boat and working out how to sail it home is our only chance. Something I be willing to lose my life attempting rather than chancing what the white skins have in store for us at journey's end."

Murmurs of agreement rippled through the shackled prisoners.

Those in a position to do so tugged at the rings fixed to the floor that their chains were fed through.

Captain Bartholomew Warren stood on the foredeck of his ship, the Hannibal, an English slaver supplying the Americas with a labor force of African Negros, with his eyes sweeping over the flotsam his vessel passed through. He watched as the largest piece yet scrape along the hull. It was the side wall and back corner of an officer's cabin from a ship's sterncastle to which, amazingly enough, two small framed portraits, one of a well-dressed woman and the other of two children, were still attached.

"It's the wreckage of a ship, but what's it doing out here? You'd normally see this kind of damage from a vessel struck against rocks or reefs, but we're many miles from any land."

Elias Myles, the first mate, scrutinized the pieces of wreckage. "I've seen signs of charring, so a sea battle's probably the cause."

"True, cannon shot could rip a ship to pieces" agreed the captain. "Pirates, you think, or the Spanish?"

"Impossible to say for certain, but pirates seem more likely with their heightened activities in these parts lately," answered Myles. He placed a spyglass to his eye and aimed it at the thick mist extending along the horizon. Glimpsing something, he focused on the patch of shadow briefly revealed before being reclaimed again by the fog. He handed his captain the telescope. "I only caught a fleeting glimpse, but I think it was a ship."

With pirates and the damn Spanish stalking these waters, Captain Warren understood his first mate's concern. There were stories of buccaneers concealing themselves in the fringes of fog banks while waiting for unsuspecting ships to come within range. They would then strike like a venomous serpent, plundering anything of value and usually killing all on board who held no worth of ransom.

The captain put the spyglass to his eye and focused on the patch of fog his first mate had indicated. Swirling mist filled his vision. He was about to remove it from his eye when something appeared, the ghostly form of a ship that at first looked as intangible as the damp fog that all but shrouded it. He concentrated the spyglass on its flapping, ripped sails, their loose lines whipping across the uninhabited deck.

The captain lowered the spyglass and turned to his first mate. "It's a ship all right, but it looks deserted."

Myles raised his eyebrows as he took the spyglass to see for himself and scanned the deserted decks. "Ghost ship?" he questioned.

The captain humphed. It was the tag that superstitious sailors attached to vessels absent any crew found drifting on the high seas. "If pirates or the Spanish didn't kill them, the crew's likely been struck down with disease—yellow fever, dysentery, scurvy or the like. It wouldn't be the first time it's happened."

The captain pondered his options. From this distance, apart from its sails, the three-master seemed in good condition. If the crew had abandoned ship for some reason or were dead or dying, something that could easily be speeded up, it would make excellent salvage for him to sell on reaching port. A ship such as that in reasonable condition would fetch a high price and would more than offset the loss of the dead slaves that they had thrown overboard.

There had been thirteen to date, and they had hardly started their journey. There would be more, disappointing but acceptable losses. Cattle and goats were hardier than these black-skinned heathens.

The captain took the spyglass from Myles. "Take a bearing on an intercept course so that I can appraise the vessel's worth as salvage."

The first mate nodded. "Aye, aye, Captain."

Contemplating his eleven percent of the profits as he went to instruct the helmsman and roust some of the crew from their slumber, Myles hoped it was a ghost ship, and it was in good condition, or at the very least had a cargo worth salvaging.

The captain and crew lined the port rail and stared at the mysterious ship they slowly approached. Only the creak of the ship's timbers and the gentle splash of waves breaking over the bow broke the uncanny silence.

"Is that seaweed around the hull?" asked Taffy Perkins, crossing himself when the bow of the three-master drew level with the bow of the Hannibal.

Boatswain, Abiah Clements, gazed down at the water around the vessel's hull and the thick mass of weed it dragged along with it. Though unsure what to make of it, like most things he didn't understand, he considered it a bad omen. He gazed down the line of sailors and signaled to the five men equipped with grappling hooks to be ready if the captain issued the order to snag her.

Captain Warren took in the sleek lines of the Dutch India ship. Unlike his patched up and worn ancient vessel, it seemed in excellent condition. Probably not more than a year or two out of the shipyard that had built it. His appreciative examination of the hull picked out the copper sheets attached below the waterline, protection against the Teredo worms that infested these warm waters, pests that were currently feasting on the hull of his ship. Commonly called shipworm, they were voracious feeders upon any timbers exposed to the sea, reducing the most robust ship to a worm-holed weakened structure with the strength of balsa wood. They had seen the demise of many ships and crew when their sponge-like hulls caved in. The copper was a recent addition by ship owners who could carry the cost, a design feature prompted when the Danish slave ship, the *Kron-Printzen*, sunk when her worm-weakened hull caved in. The loss of eight hundred and twenty slaves, precious cargo, and fifty-four of her sixty-two crew, including all its officers, was a loss its owners weren't prepared to suffer again. When Henry Wiggins, a well-renowned shipbuilder, suggested using copper sheets to protect the hull against the wood-devouring parasites, the merchants bulked at the expense for the unproven technology. To prove his theory, Wiggins went as far as to wrap a piece of timber in copper and had it towed along with another identical piece of unprotected timber behind one of the East Indiaman ships when it entered the warmer waters of the Caribbean where the worm thrived. Upon the ship's return, both pieces of wood were examined, it was found that though the unshielded timber was full of worm boreholes, the copper-sheathed one was in perfect condition. Accepting the hard-to-refute evidence, the

Hell Ship

wealthy ship owners and merchants had relented and had their ships' hulls copper-plated. They had also raised the prices of their goods and services accordingly to offset the costs.

The sailor at the tip of the forecastle called out the ship's name. "It's the Fortuyn."

"The Flying Dutchman," gasped one of the crew, crossing himself.

After glaring at the sailor, the captain turned to the first mate with a quizzical frown. "Flying Dutchman?"

"The Fortuyn was owned by the Dutch East India Company operating out of Amsterdam, the port it was headed for when it was thought ship and crew had perished in a treacherous storm encountered around the Cape of Good Hope. However, since then, there have been sightings of the Fortuyn, or the Flying Dutchman as it has commonly become known, by other ships sailing these waters. Some who have seen her have reported it as floating above the waves."

"Ah," exclaimed the captain. "Dutch ship hence the Flying Dutchman."

"In part, yes," confirmed Myles. "The name now given to the mysterious vessel could also allude to its Dutch captain, Bernard Fokke, who had an uncanny knack of making the round trip to Java weeks quicker than any other vessel. Some believed he was in league with the devil."

The captain snorted. "We'll have none of that superstitious, gullible nonsense aboard my ship."

"No, sir," replied Myles promptly.

The captain stared at the nameplate as the vessel slid by. So many ships were lost around the Cape it was hard to keep track of them all. The treacherous coastline held the nickname the Cape of Storms for a good reason. "Unless I'm looking at a mirage, it obviously didn't sink and looks in fair condition, thus a worthy prize." After scanning the empty deck, he turned to his first mate. "Give the order to seize her."

Myles took a step back and nodded when he saw the boatswain looking at him.

"Grapple her and lower the bumpers," shouted Abiah.

Those crew nearest the grapplers, cleared a space around them as three-pronged grapple irons were swung and tossed across the gap between the two ships. Other crewmen tipped tightly compressed sacks of straw over the rail, buffers to prevent the two vessels from smashing into each other.

Men hauled on the ropes tethered to the grapples and slowly the gap between the two vessels decreased. The lines were then lashed around capstans and cleats until it was secure. The tethers creaked as they strained with the ship traveling in the opposite direction, turning the Hannibal to port slightly as both vessels achieved a matching directional speed.

"Send three men over to check if anyone is onboard. If so, determine their state of health and establish the nature of the cargo if the Spanish or pirates have left us any."

Myles nodded. "Aye, Captain." He turned to the men and picked out three. "Ratcliffe, Clark and Langham, board her, look for the crew and see what's in the holds." Myles pulled the three selected men aside. "You know we'll only receive a share of the salvage prize if no one is left alive on the Fortuyn."

The three men nodded knowingly.

"We'll do that what needs to be done," assured Clark, fingering the knife at his waist.

"Good," acknowledged Myles, turning away. "Kilburn, the gangplank."

"Aye, sir," acknowledged Kilburn, and bridged the gap between the ships with the wooden plank he held ready for the task and lashed the end to the Hannibal's top rail.

Ratcliffe walked the precarious rising and falling plank first, followed by Clark and Langham.

The crew aboard the Hannibal watched the three men cross the Fortuyn's eerily empty deck and enter the stairwell through a door set in the side of the raised forecastle.

CHAPTER 12

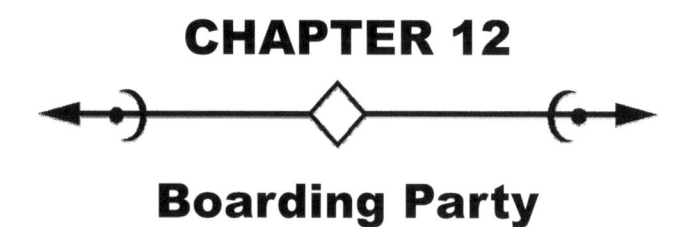

Boarding Party

On reaching the bottom of the steps, the three men gazed along the unwelcoming gloomy corridor. The oppressive atmosphere prevalent on the ship had unsettled them as soon as they had stepped aboard, and all three feared an evil presence lingered on board the vessel.

Legends of ghost ships sailing the seas looking for fresh victims were rife among sailors, a superstitious bunch prone to put their faith in doom, gloom, and apparitions. They readily believed every legend they heard connected to the sea, whether it be mermaids, giant sea creatures that attacked vessels and dragged them beneath the waves, or mysterious phantom ships that should be avoided at all costs.

Ratcliffe jumped when Langham nudged him.

"Let's be done with this quick-like so we can get off this accursed vessel before something bad happens," said Langham, voicing the concerns they all felt.

"It's just an empty ship," said Ratcliffe, unconvincingly. "Creepy, yes, but no reason for it ter be anything cursed."

"Guess we'll soon find out," said Clark.

With his two comrades following, Ratcliffe moved to the first door and peered into one of the three cramped officers' rooms that seemed luxurious compared to their smelly and crew-packed sleeping conditions. The two beds either side of the door were empty. Neatly turned-back blankets and fluffed pillows showed no signs of recent occupation.

Langham and Clark found the next two officer quarters just as deserted.

Clark pointed ahead at a dark stain on the floor, and the long splashed arc on the wall. "Is that blood?"

Ratcliffe led them forward and wiped a finger on the stain. "It's blood, but dry. Meaning it didn't happen recently, which is its only saving grace." He followed the others gaze along the blood trail leading to the galley.

Pots and pans hanging from hooks in the cooking area clanged against each other with the roll of the ship. To the anxious men, it sounded like ominous death knells warning of their impending doom.

"We should've armed ourselves with pistols afore stepping aboard," moaned Clark, glancing behind nervously when a door, set into motion by the roll of the ship, banged against its frame.

"The blood ain't fresh, so whatever was responsible is probably long gone," offered Langham.

"*Probably* don't fill me with comfort that it has," worried Clark.

They moved along to the galley and stared at the tables set with half-eaten meals never finished. If the plates, cups, cooking pots, cutlery, and spilled food on the floor weren't evidenced enough that something untoward had happened here, the blood splashes around the room were impossible to argue with.

"By the stage of food rot, it has ter be a few months old," offered Langham.

"What could've happened here to make them abandon their meal," voiced Clark, his eyes darting around nervously.

All were aware of the meager shipboard rations most sailors faced. Unless they were ill, were being attacked, or death threatened, no sailor would leave a meal unfinished, no matter how foul its taste.

"Maybe they were attacked by pirates," suggested Ratcliffe. "It would explain the blood."

Langham dragged his eyes from the trail of dripped blood leading through the galley and shook his head. "They would've taken a ship in as good condition as this or at the very least plundered anything aboard of value or use." He pointed at the food decaying in the kitchen. "Also, pirates wouldn't have left victuals behind to rot. No, whatever foulness occurred here, Buccaneers weren't responsible."

They moved through the galley, past small dry-store rooms and entered the crew quarters.

Light spread by the crystal prism set in the deck highlighted splashes of dried blood on the floor and on some of the closely hung hammocks that swung with creaky groans from the sways of the ship, evidence some of the crew had been butchered in their unconscious state. Shadows moved eerily, adding another layer of fearfulness to the scene as the three men contemplated the massacre that had evidently taken place here.

"This is bad," stated Clark. "Really, really bad. We should leave, now!"

"Calm yerself, man," ordered Langham. "If them responsible fer this bloodshed was still here, they would've attacked or revealed themselves by now."

"I still think it might be pirates," argued Ratcliffe, his head turning to every swish of rubbing hammocks, creak of wood and a bottle that rolled back and forth with each rise and fall of the wave-tossed ship. "I've heard stories about pirates luring vessels ter them with ships that look deserted. They hide and butcher anyone who comes aboard and then steals ship and cargo."

"Well, we've *come*, and we've not been attacked," pointed out Langham.

"That don't mean nothing," argued Ratcliffe. "They're probably waiting fer more of our crew ter come aboard before revealing themselves."

"Pirates didn't do this," stated Clark ominously.

The others turned to Clark and looked at the three rips in the bloodstained hammock he stared at.

"I think an animal's onboard," added Clark, spreading three fingers wide to run along each rip. "Something big and vicious."

"Better an animal than what I was imagining," uttered Ratcliffe. "An animal can be killed."

"Maybe we should go fetch some pistols before venturing farther?" suggested Clark. "Just in case…"

"Stay your fearful imaginations," ordered Langham. "I'm not willing ter suffer the captain's wrath because yer two ladies be afraid of the dark."

"It's not the dark that scares me," defended Ratcliffe, "but what it hides."

"Anyway, common sense dictates that if an animal did attack the crew, it'd be dead by now without water to slake its thirst. Come on, we've only the gundeck, hold, and bilge ter check down here and then we can return topside." As keen as his two comrades to get the job done, Langham pushed hammocks aside as he made his way through the room and down to the gundeck. Though they would prefer to be heading in the opposite direction, Clark and Ratcliffe reluctantly followed.

On entering the dark hold, the air infused with the aroma of exotic aromatic spices, Langham grabbed a lantern from a hook just inside the door and lit it. He held it high, spilling light a little way into the room. Something scuttled out of the light's far reach and went behind some stacked crates covered in rope netting secured to the floor.

"What was that?" asked Ratcliffe, grabbing Langham's arm.

Langham shook Ratcliffe's grip off. "A rat." Though he hadn't seen the creature, what else could it be?

Following the blood trails, Langham took a few steps into the hold, shifting the light left and right to search between the stacked cargo of crates, barrels, and sacks.

Glancing at the sacks wrapped in oilcloth to repel moisture and seeping heady, exotic scents, Langham turned and shone the light on his two nervous comrades. "Spices and they look dry. We'll all earn a pretty penny from this when we get the ship back ter port."

The thought of the wealth they would earn from their share of the profits lowered the men's unease slightly.

Another scampering sound, like a handful of dry twigs thrown across the wooden floor, turned them to a group of barrels a short distance away.

"That didn't sound like no rat," stated Ratcliffe, his anxiety heightened.

"Expert on rodent footsteps now, are we?" questioned Langham sarcastically, even though he agreed with Ratcliffe. "The countries this ship must have visited are filled with strange animals. We've seen some of them ourselves, any one of which could have crept aboard while it was docked. Or maybe it was brought onboard ter sell back home, and it escaped from its cage."

"It did sound small," voiced Clark, "so probably not dangerous and more frightened of us than we are of it."

"I doubt that," uttered Ratcliffe, glancing nervously back at the exit he wanted to flee through. "We've seen enough. Let's go inform the captain of what we've found."

"We still have the bilge and the stern areas to check," reminded Langham.

Ratcliffe sighed. "Then let's get it done and be gone."

With heads on a swivel for the creature they'd heard, the three men crossed to the bilge hatch set in the floor at the rear of the hold. Their nervous attention focused on the bloodstained boards around the trap and the trails leading into the small gap around its edges.

Handing Ratcliffe the lantern, Langham knelt and reached for the large iron ring in the middle of the trapdoor's front edge.

Ratcliffe grabbed Langham's outstretched arm. "Yer really gonna look in there with all the blood indicating whatever yer gonna see inside is likely gonna haunt yer sleeping hours 'till the day yer die?"

"Thanks, I'm less keen to do so now, but we need to find out what happened to the crew and if anyone's hiding."

Clark snorted. "We know what happened. They're dead. That's obvious by all the blood."

"If I don't look, the captain will send us back down again," explained Langham. We're here now, so…"

"Well, I ain't looking," stated Ratcliffe, taking a step back. "I've enough nightmare material in me head without adding more horrifying images."

"I'm not so keen either," added Clark.

Langham rolled his eyes. "Then I'll look, *ladies*."

From a short distance away, the two men watched Langham grip the iron ring and heave the hatch open. He gagged and turned his head aside when the cloying stench of rotten corpses whooshed over him.

Clark and Ratcliffe clamped hands over their mouths and noses when the reek assaulted them.

"I think we've found the crew," said Clark, his voice muffled by the hand he dared not remove from his nose and mouth.

"What's left of them," added Ratcliffe. "By that stench, they ain't gonna look pretty."

Langham shoved the hatch back to rest against the side of the hull, placed the crook of his elbow over his nose and mouth, and peered into the dark hole. After a few moments, he reached a hand towards Ratcliffe. "Lantern."

Keeping his face turned away from the hole lest he glimpsed its contents, Ratcliffe handed Langham the lantern and stepped back.

Though fearing the horrible sight he was about to witness, Langham lowered the lantern into the bilge and peered inside. Bodies, mostly bones with scraps of clothes and lumps of torn, ragged flesh clinging to them, floated and bobbed in the churning, black bilge water slopping back and forth. Fighting down the bile rising in his throat, Langham leaned deeper through the hatch to do a body count. He had reached sixteen when a group of limb-and-bone-linked corpses spurted from the water and fell back with a splash that raised a fresh wave of disgusting foulness.

Terrified by the horrific creature that erupted from the slimy foulness, Langham's frightened gaze took in the glossy wet, evil monster. Whatever it was he knew it couldn't be anything God had created. Though his senses told him to flee, his fear held him there. Langham trembled when the abomination against all that was holy screeched and moved closer, sending out ripples that bumped bones and partially-eaten corpses against each other. Bloated pale faces of the dead observed the clawed hand reaching for the stranger on their ship.

Dread rippled through Clark and Ratcliffe when something beneath the boards they stood on screeched an inhuman cry. They staggered back in fright when a claw shot from the hatch, hooked Langham around the neck and yanked him inside, taking the lantern with him.

Recovering from his scare, Clark rushed to the hatch to help his friend. The sight of the gruesome corpses swirling in the brackish bilge water was highlighted by the bobbing lantern's orange glow, but there was no sign of Langham or what had grabbed him. He started when Ratcliffe appeared at his side and tugged at his arm.

Hell Ship

"We need to leave! Something devilish is down here," urged Ratcliffe, his fearful gaze focused on the eerie scuttling sounds of unknown things in the darkness around them.

It was all the encouragement Clark needed. The men rushed through the gloom to the exit. Scampering limbs homed in on them.

Clark screamed when something landed on his back. He screamed again when sharp things pierced his skin. Another creature fell on his head and stabbed claws into his face, aiming for his eyes. Clark grabbed at the spindly limbs slicing his face to the bone, yanked it free and flung it away.

Ratcliffe whimpered in terror when Clark screamed behind him. Fearing he would freeze if he turned and witnessed what was attacking his friend, he looked longingly at the dim light spilling in from the gun deck — only a few steps to go. He yelped when the foul creature with six crab-like limbs struck his head and slashed out, slicing his cheek. Grabbing its bulbous body as its limbs sought for a purchase around his face, he pulled it off and chucked it to the floor. It quickly righted itself and turned its evil eyes at him. Ratcliffe stamped on it as he sprinted past. Its body and limbs cracked with the sound of dry leaves crunching, splattering dark goo across the boards. Ratcliffe skidded to a halt at the door, spun to pull it closed and looked inside to see how his friend fared.

Clark faltered when three more creatures leaped upon him. Stabbing him with their claws, they sent him stumbling to the floor.

He raised his head in Ratcliffe's direction, both his eyes a pulpy bloody mess. "Help me."

Spying more of the vicious creatures moving towards his fallen friend, Ratcliffe could see only one outcome; Clark was beyond any help he could give him. He guiltily began to pull the door shut. A screech from across the room halted him. He gazed into the darkness at the red eyes that rose from the bilge hatch. Hard quick taps on the floor accompanied the movement of the eyes towards him. The thing that had taken Langham was coming.

In fear of his life, Ratcliffe went to close the door fully when one of the smaller creatures leaped for the narrow gap and became trapped between door and frame, preventing it from closing. Ratcliffe yanked the door hard, crunching the creature's limbs, but still it wouldn't close. A large three-fingered claw appeared around the edge, jerked the handle from Ratcliffe's grip and ripped the door from its hinges.

Ratcliffe dodged the claw that swiped at him through the doorway and fled. Barely able to control his panic, he rushed through the gundeck, up the steps and barged through the swinging hammocks with the creature on his tail. He sprinted through the galley and along the corridor. When a fresh surge of adrenaline was produced by the harrowing claws clacking on the floor in pursuit, he directed it to his pumping legs. Hope surged through him when he glimpsed the steps lit by daylight streaming through the open deck door.

While waiting for the three men to return with their report, the captain and first mate discussed their good fortune at finding the abandoned vessel.

"If pirates aren't responsible for the ship's perceived abandonment, and she was on her way home, she could hold a valuable cargo, maybe even spices and coffee," said Myles to his captain.

"My thoughts are occupied with the very same notion," replied Captain Warren, running an appraising eye over the ship. It was newer and in far better condition than the ancient vessel he commanded. His share of the prize money when they got it back to port would be considerable. He knew the crew would have already worked out their share of the salvage prize so would be just as keen to save it. "Even if the hold is empty, the ship's in fair condition and will fetch a lucrative price if we can sail her back to port."

Myles nodded his agreement. "The sails will need some work, but a skeleton crew should be able to handle her."

A commotion aboard the Fortuyn directed their attention upon Ratcliffe rushing from below screaming, his clothes splattered with blood, a gash on his cheek. "Cut her loose! Cut her loose! The devil's coming!"

The captain, his second-in-command and the crew on deck, confused by the man's obvious terror and screamed demands, watched Ratcliffe sprint to the Fortuyn's port side and jump onto the rail. Ignoring the gangplank spanning the gap between the two tethered vessels, he leaped across to the Hannibal.

The captain strode briskly over to the man spilled on the deck. Ratcliffe's skin was as white as the sails, and he had a look of fright etched on his face such as the captain had never laid eyes on before. "What happened and where are Langham and Clark?"

"They're dead, Captain. Ripped apart by the devils on that accursed ship. I beg yer, Captain, yer must give the order ter cut Hannibal free before it's too late and we're all slaughtered."

Warren shot his surrounding crew a steely gaze when some crossed themselves and worried murmurs of the devil coming to get them babbled through them. When their nervous prattling had again fallen to silence, he glanced at the entrance to the Fortuyn's forward hold that the three men had entered a short while before. Unwilling to give up the prize so easily, he returned his attention to the terrified crewman. Something had obviously scared the man, but a devil? Not on his watch. It wasn't unusual for officers to bring exotic animals onboard from the lands they visited to sell or impress their friends with back home. It was probably one of these more dangerous species the captain or an officer had collected, and it had escaped. Although he doubted that would explain the deserted ship unless—impossible as it sounded—the dangerous beast had killed and devoured them all.

"Could it not have been a lion or tiger that attacked you?" inquired the captain.

Ratcliffe shook his head. "Weren't no cat and there's more than one of 'em. Six or seven were quite small but no less vicious, but the worst is a large evil one that killed Langham and almost got me." He cast a frightened gaze back at the Fortuyn. "I didn't get a good look as it was dark down there, but I knows they weren't no lions or tigers. They've got spindly limbs with claws long and razor sharp which they swished and slashed something deadly. The larger, different one had eyes terrifying to gaze into. They looked straight into your soul, tainting it with its evil. If that weren't bad enough, they're so fast they sliced through me mates before they hardly knew they were there. I only survived because I was nearest the exit. I tell yer, Captain, and I begs that yer believe me, those things dwelling on that ship must have escaped from Hell, and if we don't cut it free, they'll soon be on this one, and then we'll all suffer the same fate of Clark and Langham."

When Ratcliffe's babbling ceased, murmurs of disquiet and fear rippled through the crew, all too ready to believe and act upon their frightened crewmate's warning.

The captain's stern gaze that threatened a flogging for any insubordination again swept over them, bringing them to an anxious silence. "What about the cargo and Fortuyn's crew?"

"Spices and a hold full of cargo, but its crew are as dead as me shipmates. What was left of them was in the bilge. It wasn't a sight I'm ever likely ter forget, and the stench…"

In an unprecedented act of kindness, the captain placed a hand on Ratcliffe's shoulder. "Head below and tell cook I said to give you a large tot of rum and then rest awhile." As Ratcliff headed below, Warren selected four nearby men. "Arm yourselves and go kill these damn beasts, whatever they are."

Though anxious about the task they had been given, they feared the Captain's wrath more than any perceived devil aboard the ghost ship.

"Aye, aye, Captain."

The chief mate was on his way to collect pistols from the arms locker but halted when the captain called out to him.

"Elias, take two men with you and bring extra weapons, powder and shot to hand out to the crew just in case whatever animal is aboard, makes its way topside."

"Aye, Captain." Selecting two men to accompany him, Myles headed below.

They returned a short while later and dished out the weapons.

Watched by the captain and crew, the four chosen men loaded their weapons. Matner drew his cutlass and led the others to the gangplank and cautiously boarded the Fortuyn. Halting at the bow entrance, Frank Matner gazed below, his pistol held shakily out ready to fire. The top step creaked when he stood on it and crouched to peer along the gloom-ridden corridor.

He turned to one of the men behind him and sheathed his sword. "Adams, fetch me a lantern and light it."

The man went to do Matner's bidding and returned a few moments later with two lamps. He handed one to Matner and kept the other.

Lowering the light below and spying it free of any threat, Matner descended and waited for his three reluctant shipmates to join him.

Making hardly a sound, they crept towards the galley. They found splashes and trails of old blood but nothing responsible for Ratcliffe's terror. They entered the sleeping quarters and spread out in a line as they moved to the steps leading to the gundeck and the ship's hold.

Matner took in the broken door at the far end of the gundeck he cautiously approached and aimed the lantern light inside the hold. He focused on the fresh bloodstains and then on something squashed on the floor. He stepped inside and crouched beside it while the others roamed their anxious gazes and weapons around the room crowded with stores and cargo. Matner prodded the crushed carcass with the pistol barrel. He had never seen anything like it. Its six limbs could indicate it was some type of strange crab, but it was like no crustacean he'd ever encountered in all his years at sea. Gills on the sides of its bulbous head were another strangeness attributed to the vicious-looking sea creature. He stood and looked around the stocked hold filled with the reek of expensive aromatic spices and something far less pleasant coming from the open hatch at the far end of the room.

The others followed his slow walk towards it.

Following at the rear, David O'Keefe glanced behind at a sound. Relieved to find nothing there, he turned back. Claw-tipped limbs stabbed him through the neck and lifted him from his feet. The pistol slipped from his grasp.

When something warm splattered the back of his neck, Adams glanced behind and frowned at the pistol clattering to the floor. Spying no sign of O'Keefe, he held the lantern out to shed light on the surroundings, but he was nowhere to be seen. After noticing something splattering on the floor, blood, he gazed up to where a large creature was hanging with O'Keefe impaled on one of its clawed limbs. Movement around the animal directed his terrified gaze upon the ceiling alive with smaller, but no less terrifying, creatures—many more than the six or seven Ratcliffe had reported.

Adams screamed when some of the small creatures dropped towards him. He dodged back, barging into Spelman, knocking him off balance. Adams fired a wild shot, killing one of his vicious attackers; the others landed on his chest and dug in their claws. He panicked and swung the lantern at the creatures clawing at him. Oil spilled from the lamp, splashed the beasts, his chest, and face and whooshed into flame. The burning creatures squealed but didn't release their grip. Adams screamed as the flames consumed them and him. Screaming in agony, he dropped the lantern and flapped at the flames with burning hands.

Matner spun. Seeing Adams aflame, he grabbed a canvas cover from a stack of dry goods and placed it over the man, extinguishing the flames that would have destroyed the precious cargo and ship. He switched his scared gaze to the creatures scuttling over the ceiling and dropping to the floor, then at the larger, sleeker version that fell holding O'Keefe's limp form.

Matner glanced at Adams, wracked with pain and then at Spelman backing away, terror etched on his face as he stared at the monstrosities surrounding him. Without the time to reload, the one shot in his pistol wouldn't help him. Matner aimed his at the giant creature and fired as a smaller one leaped into his line of sight. The lead ball entered the small creature and deflected the shot, taking out another of its brethren before the ball buried itself in the ceiling. Matner flipped the pistol over and holding it like a club drew his sword. A shot beside him rang out, and a still smoking pistol skidded across the floor. He turned his head. Spelman flopped to the floor; the hole in his head had provided him with a quicker death than that offered by the monsters, as well as a more pain-free one. He was on his own.

Matner was knocked off his feet when the large creature threw O'Keefe's corpse at him. Both crashed to the floor. Matner turned his face to the awful stench that battled the spicy aroma for dominance in the room, overpowering now, and peered into the bilge. Bodies, bloated and rotten, floated in the foul water. Scampering claws spurred him to his feet. He stamped on one about to jump onto his leg, knocked aside another dropping from the ceiling with the pistol and stabbed at another with the sword. There were too many to fight. He sprinted to the side and nipped around the end of the tightly packed stores. He threw the pistol at one that dashed for him, breaking one of its long arms, and sidled through the narrow gap between hull, crates, and barrels. Some of the smaller creatures followed. Others climbed over the stacks of cargo. If he could reach the end and dash for the exit, he might survive.

Spurting along, he reached the end and squeezed past a curved hull beam. Stepping into a gap between the cargo, he came face to face with the massive creature squeezed into the space, waiting for him. A limb shot out. Matner swiped the sword at it, knocking it aside with a clash of steel on scales. Scampering of small legs behind gave him seconds to act. He threw the sword. It bounced off the giant creature's head and slid along its scaly body before dropping to the floor. It retreated. Sprinting through the gap, Matner ducked around the claws swiping at him when he rushed past. Ducking and dodging the lethal claws, he ran for the exit and entered the gun deck. A glance behind revealed monstrosities large, medium, and small in pursuit, their shrieks, and snarls filling the ship. Matner sprinted through the gun deck and up the steps at its end. Scuttling of the monsters behind gaining on him heightened his fear. He barged through the hammocks, leaving them swinging and creaking in his wake. His heart pounded. His body trembled.

A glance behind revealed the giant creature was almost close enough to swipe its claws down his back. He stumbled on the pots and pans covering the galley floor but managed to keep his footing. The creature also slipped on the cooking utensils, slowing it slightly when it crashed into a table. Matner's look ahead picked out daylight streaming through the doorway to the top deck. Confident that if he could reach the Hannibal and the armed crew he'd be safe, Matner thought through the actions he needed to survive. *Leap up the steps. Rush across the deck while warning his crewmates of the danger. Jump onto the Hannibal and help the others cut the grapple ropes while those with weapons killed as many of the creatures as they could.*

He placed a foot on the bottom step and leaped up them. He screamed when claws stabbed through his shin, spilling him painfully to the treads, his top half extended through the door. Aware his plan had failed, Matner looked at the captain and the crew lining the Hannibal's rail staring at him.

"Flee! There's no salvation here." He screamed when he was dragged back through the doorway.

When Matner's screams were cut short, blood sprayed from the doorway and splattered across the deck. Staring fearfully at the entrance where they all expected the thing responsible for slaughtering Matner to emerge, the crew gasped when his corpse, its skin shredded, shot out and skidded across the deck, leaving a blood trail in its wake. Their terrified gazes flicked back to the doorway when a snarl, deep and menacing, heralded the appearance of Matner's killer.

The front limb stretched from the opening and stabbed a claw into the deck with a splintering thwack. The second limb was followed by its vicious head, which turned and looked at them as it hauled its terrifying form onto the deck. Tentacles on its back turned their tips towards the men on the Hannibal and chomped their teeth menacingly. Seemingly unperturbed by their numbers, it snarled at them when it skulked closer to the Fortuyn's rail and them, sending some of the Hannibal's crew retreating in terror.

When a wave of smaller crab-like creatures poured from the doorway, the captain was shaken from his shock. "Shoot the damn things and cut us free!" he yelled.

As weapons were fired, men armed with axes and knives rushed to the tethers and chopped through them.

Though some of the smaller creatures were killed or wounded, the bigger beast was so fast at dodging the shots it remained unscathed.

"They're coming!" someone screamed.

As the crew frantically reloaded their weapons, the smaller creatures raced to the rail. Keen to taste the fresh prey on offer, they leaped across the gap between the two ships and attacked.

The larger creature observed the human slaughter that ensued.

Witnessing the merciless creatures' attack on his men, the terrified captain backed away before they turned on him. Realizing Matner was right when he said there was no salvation here, his thoughts turned to survival. Grabbing his first mate's arm to drag his frightened gaze from the carnage that would soon come their way, he issued his orders, "If we remain on the ship, we're all doomed! Grab some men and launch a landing boat. It's our only chance."

Myles selected those around him, and together they set about hoisting the small landing craft over the side. As they began lowering it to the sea, the captain and first mate climbed in. As soon as it hit the waves, the crew released the lines and slid down the ropes into the boat. Terror drove them to abandon their surviving crewmates. They grabbed the oars and started rowing away from the Hannibal.

Wondering how the men that had boarded the Fortuyn had fared, Ratcliffe lay in his hammock listening to the events unfolding on deck. Though he hoped the men who'd gone aboard the ghost ship had killed the devilish creatures, his experiences with the horrors pictured a different outcome. They should cut the cursed vessel free, sail away to a safe distance and use the cannons to blow it out of the water and send the demons back to whatever hell from whence they'd come.

Muffled pistol shots from deep within the Fortuyn indicated the fight had started, then shortly after, Matner's voice rang out.

"Flee! There's no salvation here."

Shots from above rang out."

Screams soon followed.

Hearing the commotion that followed topside and the shots that indicated the creatures had shown themselves, Ratcliffe listened for a few anxious moments before climbing from his hammock. If the beasts were attacking, his shipmates would need all the help they could get. He headed along the corridor and ascended the steps to the forecastle.

Ratcliffe shivered in fear when he stepped onto the deck and gazed around at the massacre taking place. Creatures had swarmed aboard the Hannibal and were attacking the men. All were doomed. Men, dead and dying, already littered the bloodied boards, and all were being feasted upon. Ratcliffe glanced at his comrades still on their feet fighting battles they couldn't possibly win and then dodged back into the doorway when the large creature leaped from the quarterdeck above him and thudded to the deck. As soon as it landed, it rushed forward a short distance and lowered its head to a gap in the deck. It then started ripping at the boards, sending chunks of wood and splinters flying.

Lit by slithers of light seeping through the gaps in the deck boards badly in need of maintenance, the slaves gazed aloft. Aware something that had the crew rattled was going on above them, the slaves trapped in the dark hold listened to the frantic, shouted orders they couldn't understand.

"Oh, my God, what is that?"

"It's the devil!"

Pistol shots.

Panicked footsteps on deck boards.

"They're coming!"

Multiple screams. Clacking of things scuttling across the deck. Bodies thudded to the boards. Blood dripped through uncaulked gaps onto the slaves.

Some of the captives began to panic. Women and children sobbed.

Chains clanked through the hold as men desperately tried to yank them free of the floor fixings.

The screams and footsteps faded.

Except for the creaking of timbers, ominous silence fell over the ship.

The shackled captives' frightened gazes followed the numerous sets of click-clacking footsteps across the boards as unknown terrible things moved about. A man gasped when the tip of a curved black claw slipped through a board joint, and bright eyes lowered to the gap.

"The dev…" a man began to utter fearfully, wrenching at his restraint furiously.

The man beside him quickly slipped an arm around the man's face and smothered his mouth, holding him still. "Quiet, you'll bring it down ter us," he whispered.

With fear-filled eyes, the man calmed enough for the man restraining him to risk removing his arm when the eyes moved away.

"What's happening, Martaigo?" whispered Jonus, his frightened eyes staring at foul beings interrupting the light rays as they crisscrossed the deck.

Martaigo shrugged. "Nothing good fer us."

A series of smaller scuttles across the boards were followed by the gruesome sounds of the creatures feasting upon their fallen victims littering the deck. Blood dripped onto those directly below the carnage.

Martaigo silenced the whimpering of a ten-year-old boy with a stern look and a finger to his lips.

Zumba, who had been heaving continuously at his restraints where he was shackled a row in front of Martaigo, reached down and slipped his fingers under the metal plate the chain on his side ran through. As his fingertips probed the moist timber, they grazed the tip of a stout nail that had almost pulled free. He turned to Martaigo. "My ring is almost free. The boards are more rotten here."

Martaigo stood as tall as the cramped space and the chains looped through the iron rings attached to the floor would allow, and looked at the metal plate raised on one side. His eyes flicked to the ring of two keys hanging on a hook by the steps leading above. If Zumba could free himself from the floor and reach the keys, they might stand a chance against whatever threat had attacked their captors. He turned to Zumba. "Quietly as yer can, try and free yourself and go for the keys."

Zumba nodded and set about hauling on the metal plate.

Martaigo gazed around at his frightened comrades and whispered, "It's important we all be silent. The slightest noise could attract whatever demons are up there down ter us. Zumba is almost free. If he succeeds, everyone this side of the chain must feed our slack to him. If he can reach the keys, he'll unlock our chains."

"And what we do then?" asked Martha, cuddling a twelve-year-old girl, snatched when she was collecting water from a stream near her village.

Martaigo tilted his head to the boards when something clacked ominously across them. "We hope whatever devils killed the white-skins leave. If they do, we work out how ter sail this ship back ter our lands. If they don't, then we fight them as best we can and hope enough of us survive because with the crew dead and none ter give us provisions, we are sure ter perish if we remain here.

A splintering of wood directed everyone's gaze at Zumba holding aloft the ring the chain binding all on that side together was fed through. A padlock at the end secured the chain to another ring in the floor. Once unlocked they would be able to pull the chain through the other floor rings and their shackles and be free.

"Well done, Zumba," praised Martaigo quietly. "Now go for the keys."

Everyone linked to Zumba's chain, quietly fed their slack to the person in front until their shackled shins were halted by the rusty iron rings attached at intervals to the floor.

Zumba pulled up the slack and fed out the chain as he crawled towards the end wall. It pulled taut too far away for him to reach the keys with his hands. The chain-attached captives grimaced when Zumba strained against the iron tether, forcing their ankles tight against the metal rings. It was no good, Zumba was still a little short. He changed tactics and lay on his back with his shackled arms stretched over his head. Splinters dug into his skin when he squirmed closer to the wall and walked his feet up to the keys. With one foot pressed against the wall for support, he tried to grip the keys with the toes of his other foot. Feeling his toes wrapping around the cold metal gave him the confidence he could do it. He carefully lifted the ring off the hook and was about to lower it to the floor when it slipped from his grip and crashed to the floor with a metallic clang.

A loud thump on the boards was swiftly followed by footsteps clacking speedily across the deck when whatever foul creature had heard homed in on the noise. Zumba gasped when red eyes, evil and devilish, peered through a gap at him. The thing screeched and began stabbing and ripping its claws at the wood.

Dragging his eyes away from the splintering boards he feared the creature would soon be through, Martaigo looked at Zumba. "Grab keys," he called out urgently.

Fighting his panic, Zumba pulled the key ring closer with a foot until it was within reach of his hand. He knelt and threw it to the man nearest the padlock.

As splinters and small chunks of wood dropped to the floor, Gingada frantically fumbled a key into the padlock and found the correct one on his first try.

A section of deck clattered to the floor.

All eyes turned to the monstrous head pressed to the splintered hole and its evil eyes sweeping over them.

Women screamed. Children cried. Men recoiled in fear.

The creature pulled its head away and screeched a command.

Gingada twisted the key. The padlock sprung open. He unhooked the lock and dropped it to the floor. "Chain is free," he called out as he released his shackles from it.

Immediately, those on the same line frantically pulled the chain through the loops.

Zumba watched the chain pulled by those on the line behind him whizzing through his shackles. As soon as he was free, he crawled away from the hole that lighter and smaller click-clacks converged on. Things barely glimpsed when they dropped through the dim light thudded to the floor as he cowered beneath the steps.

Claws clacked lightly on the boards as the horrors gazed around at their prey and moved through the gloom.

Gingada screamed when something landed on his shoulder and dug into his skin. He grabbed it and threw it into the darkness. Two more took its place and sliced at his flesh. Others rushed to the scent of blood. Screaming in agony from the hellish demons clawing at his body, Gingada struck his head hard on the ceiling. He took three unsteady steps before the creatures brought him down and five breaths before he breathed his last.

Screams of terror and pain filled the hold when the creatures moved amongst the captives to feed. Chains clanked as the prisoners desperately fought to be free from their shackles.

Aware he needed to get off the ship before he was spotted, Ratcliffe tore his eyes away from the massive creature ripping at the deck, sending chunks of wood and splinters flying, and gazed around for an escape route. He noticed the empty space previously occupied by a landing boat, which indicated someone had abandoned ship. He shot a glance at the giant creature when it screeched a shrill call and was surprised when many of the smaller animals rushed to the hole in the deck and dropped through. The creatures remaining thankfully seemed more interested in ripping flesh from corpses than in what was going on around them. None looked his way as he crossed to the quarterdeck steps.

Hearing terrible, fear-filled screams coming from the human cargo below, he glanced at the locked, crisscross slatted hatch to the hold that dark hands poked through. The trap was an exit for the stench of sweat, piss, and feces but not the prisoners that caused it. There was no hope for those below now. More worried about his own life than the slaves, Ratcliffe climbed up to the quarterdeck and rushed to the rail. About thirty yards away the captain, the first mate and four crew rowed away in the missing landing boat.

Worried he would be trapped aboard with the deadly creatures if he didn't make his move, Ratcliffe had just stepped back from the rail to get a run up to dive over the side when five animals rushed up the steps and headed straight for him. He grabbed a lantern hanging from a hook and threw it at them. It smashed on contact with the deck, splashing the creatures with burning oil. The flames licked at the boards and began spreading. Ratcliffe shot a glance at further animals, drawn by the commotion, who were heading for him. He was running out of time. He sprinted for the starboard rail and dived over.

Two terrified men hiding behind water barrels watched Ratcliffe leap over the side of the ship, and believing a watery grave would be preferable to what they faced if they remained on board, they decided to copy him. They emerged from their hiding place, rushed to the rail and leaped overboard.

Before they entered the water, tendrils shot out from the weed heading for the small boat and plucked them from the air. Their screams were choked to silence by seawater pouring into their mouths when they were dragged beneath the waves.

Ratcliffe shot a glance back at the screams and noticed the weed tendrils reaching for him. Increasing his pace, he swam for the small boat.

The men in the boat watching the flames consume the Hannibal and listening to the faint screams of all those trapped aboard had witnessed Ratcliffe's leap into the sea and held the boat steady as they waited for him to catch up.

When two more crew leaped overboard and were snatched by the tendrils, the first mate pointed out the weed moving purposefully towards Ratcliffe and them.

Shouting warnings to Ratcliffe to hurry, they shared their gazes between the swimming man and a few creatures that had spotted him leaping from the Hannibal into the sea.

As those around him screamed and tried unsuccessfully to fight off the devils, Zumba fought against his rising panic. Fearing the creatures would discover him, he trembled at the bright eyes moving through the gloom. It was a terrible, nightmarish sight. Ignoring those suffering around him, self-preservation drove him from his hiding place.

"Zumba, the key!" called out the woman on the end of the opposite line the creatures had miraculously passed by.

Zumba could barely make out the woman in the darkness pointing desperately at the floor a short distance away. Spying the object of her attention, he darted forward, kicked the padlock with the key still in it across to the woman and bolted up the stairs. He shoved a shoulder against the locked door and stumbled through when it crashed open. Spying daylight and the steps highlighted in its welcoming glow a short distance away, he rushed up them and took deep gulps of fresh air when he stepped onto the deck. Crackling flames creeping along the ship highlighted his terrified gaze as he took in the ravaged, bloody bodies and the giant monster peering through the hole in the deck at its smaller feeding brethren he had just escaped from.

Guiltily ignoring the screams of terror and pain coming from below of those he couldn't help, Zumba silently backed over to the small boat on the opposite side of the ship from the flames. It was his only chance. When he bumped into it, he turned and glanced at the ropes. He needed to work out how to get it in the water.

Blood sprayed from his mouth when the clawed limb that had entered his lower back pushed through his insides and erupted from his chest. Lifted off his feet and dragged closer to the monstrosity that had impaled him, Zumba stared into the eyes of his killer and then its jaws when it shifted him towards its gaping, teeth-lined mouth.

When it had finished feasting, the patriarch flung Zumba's remains to the deck, descended the steps Zumba had recently fled up and entered the hold filled with the screams of terrified humans. Its gills fluttered in anticipation when it breathed in their fear. It gazed around at the human feast its offspring had started devouring and peered at the screaming and crying food crowded in a trembling mass at the back. It headed deeper into the room to claim its next meal.

When the flames began encroaching on the lower decks and threatened to cut off their exit, the patriarch screeched an order to flee and joined its brethren climbing out. They leaped into the sea and swam towards the ship they had made their home.

"They're abandoning ship," said the first mate, pointing out the swimming creatures. "Maybe when the Fortuyn's drifted away to a safe distance we can re-board the Hannibal. If we can't save her, perhaps we can salvage some provisions before the flames, and the sea claim her?"

As the captain's reply formed on his lips, the Hannibal exploded with a thundering boom that sprayed burning timbers high into the heavens, evidence the flames had reached the gunpowder store.

As wreckage splashed around them, the captain and first mate hauled Ratcliffe into the boat, and the others set to rowing again.

Captain Warren turned his gaze away from his sinking ship and observed some of the creatures climbing back aboard the Fortuyn. He focused on the giant monster that had jumped onto the quarterdeck and stood there like a proud captain.

"They're still coming for us," called out Myles, pointing at the strange weed heading for them and the four creatures climbing on top, where they perched and snarled and shrieked at them.

"Row us away from that weed and damned hell ship before they reach us," ordered the captain.

The four men at the oars rowed quickly and forcefully, swiftly putting distance between them and the oncoming weed and its vicious passengers.

Seeming to realize they couldn't catch their prey, the weed turned around and headed back to the cursed Dutchman.

Gazing at the Hannibal, officers and crew watched as the remains of its burning hulk slipped beneath the waves with a hiss of extinguished timbers, carrying any aboard that had survived the savage onslaught to a watery grave.

Astounded by what he had just heard, Tom watched the man top up his tankard and drain it in one go.

"Without any water or provisions, we were lucky to make it ter land before we perished."

"And you reported your…encounter with these sea monsters ter the authorities?" inquired Tom.

The man snorted. "We tried, but no one believed us. Told us hunger, thirst, and the scorching sun had addled our brains."

Tom wasn't surprised by the news. If he hadn't seen the foul creatures with his own eyes, he doubted he would have believed the story either. "I assume by that scar yer wear that yer be Ratcliffe."

Ratcliffe fingered the red mark on his cheek, remembering how he received it. He pushed the nightmare image away and nodded. "Aye, Samuel Ratcliffe, that be me."

"Well, Samuel, it's an incredible tale, but I can tell by yer anxious demeanor as yer re-experienced it that it happened just as yer described."

Ratcliffe nodded his appreciation. "It's harrowing enough to belay any embellishment and something that'll haunt me fer the rest of me days."

The barkeep arrived with Ratcliff's meal and a full bottle of rum, which he set on the table. The haggard sailor wasted no time in tucking in.

When the barkeep had gone, Tom climbed from his seat. "Thanks again, Samuel. I know it can't have been easy reliving the horrific events."

Ratcliffe nodded at the fresh bottle of rum. "It wasn't, but that'll help."

"I must go, or I'll miss my passage. May good luck be your mistress, Samuel."

"Aye, I could do with some, right enough, luck and a mistress, and the same ter yer, lad."

Tom placed some coins on the table. "To help yer forget."

Ratcliffe scooped up the coins, slipped them in a pocket and watched Tom head out the exit. After another generous gulp of rum, he continued his meal

---

Believe my tale or not, and I understand if it is the latter—if I had not witnessed the nightmarish events, I too would be skeptical of its authenticity—my story you have just read is the truth.

This then is almost the end of my story.

I arrived in Amsterdam a few months later and almost immediately bought passage aboard a vessel heading to England. I never went to sea again.

I visited my parents in Somerset but withheld the true nature of my adventures, telling them a sailor's life was not for me, and that I had indeed banished the thirst for adventure from my mind. I shared with them a small part of the proceeds from selling some of Captain Trent's treasure, which I said was my share of the salvage proceeds from a ship we found adrift at sea.

Almost a year later, I left home.

By selling off Captain Trent's jewels a little at a time so as not to arouse suspicion, I was able to live a comfortable life in London. I purchased a house on the outskirts, married four years later and started a family.

I never revealed to a soul about what happened aboard the Fortuyn.

Over the following years when I read or heard about sightings of the mysterious ghost ship, the Flying Dutchman, I recalled the terrible moments and prayed for the souls taken by the devilish creatures.

It is time for me to say goodbye and that I hope you never experience anything as dreadful as I did aboard the hell ship, the Fortuyn.

May all your dreams be unburdened from fright,

Tom Hardy

CHAPTER 13

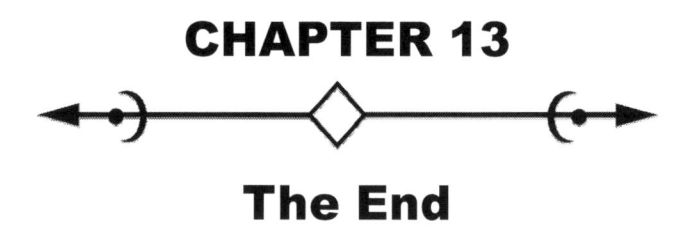

The End

Rushing down the subway escalator, Vince apologized to those he barged past. Almost tripping in his rush when he stepped from moving escalator to static floor, he headed for the platform. Turning sideways he squeezed through the rapidly narrowing gap of the closing train doors. Relieved he had made it, he walked towards the back of the carriage and slumped into a seat as the train pulled out of the station.

Feeling drowsy, he rubbed the sleep from his eyes with his fingers. He glanced at the lights flashing on and off as the train rattled over the rails. It was nothing unusual. When he heard screams coming from farther along the carriage, he tilted his head to the side and focused his gaze along the aisle. A woman slammed against the door that connected Vince's carriage to the next one. Blood streamed down her face and the window. She toppled to the ground when the door opened, and creatures he recognized from the Flying Dutchman poured through the door. Passengers screamed in terror and leaped from their seats. They were knocked to the floor screaming, dying, when creatures pounced on them. Terrified, and wondering how it was possible, Vince sat frozen as the creatures leaped across the backs of the seats and bounded along the aisle. When one jumped at his face with claws outstretched, teeth chomping, he screamed.

"Sir, are you okay?"

Shaken from the nightmare by the hand on his shoulder, Vince looked at the train guard and nodded. "Sorry, bad dream."

"It must have been," said the guard. "You were screaming like you were being murdered."

A little embarrassed, Vince glanced at the nearby passengers staring at him. "Sorry, everybody," he apologized. He turned back to the guard. "I'm a horror writer, and sometimes my stories cross over into my dreams."

"Really? Anything I might have read? I like a bit of horror."

Vince reeled off a few of his book titles to the guard's blank expression.

"Nope, ain't read any of them. Any good, are they?"

"I like to think so," replied Vince.

"I'll look out for them then."

"Appreciated," said Vince, as the guard moved on.

When the train pulled to a stop at Warren Street underground station, Vince disembarked and made his way to University College London Hospital a short distance away. After taking the elevator to the oncology department he had visited many times over the past few weeks, he spoke to a nurse and was taken to a room.

Saddened by the depressing sight of Elizabeth Hardy, now frail, bald and sickly, Vince returned her weak smile. He had visited her a few times at home and here when she had taken a turn for the worse so she could read the chapters of his book more or less as he finished them. Though she was still undergoing treatment, the outlook grew dimmer with the passing of each day. Cancer was a relentless killer.

"I hope your presence here means you've finally finished the last few chapters?" she said, adding a smile.

Glancing around at the range of medical equipment Lizzy was connected to, which seemed to have increased since his last visit, Vince sat in the chair beside the bed. "I'm pleased to report I have." He pulled a book from his pocket and handed it to her. "Here's your advance copy. It's only a print on demand copy I cobbled together as the official paperback won't be ready for a few weeks, but I thought you'd like to see Tom's story in book form."

Elizabeth studied the cover and read aloud the title. "Hell Ship – The Flying Dutchman. The true account of the catastrophic events aboard the Fortuyn as witnessed by Tom Hardy, the sole survivor of the aforementioned vessel. "I like it, and I see you've included Tom's original title."

"My agent and publisher weren't keen due to its wordiness, but as I thought it fitting that it should be included, I insisted."

"I approve." Elizabeth opened the book and smiled. "You've dedicated it to Tom and me. Thank you." She turned to the chapters she hadn't yet read and started reading.

Content to wait, Vince sat back and relaxed.

Hell Ship

Night had arrived when Vince awoke to a hand on his arm. He sat up, and turning to Elizabeth, he brushed his hair back with a hand. "Sorry. I've had a few late nights trying to finish the book before…"

She squeezed his arm. "No need to apologize. You looked so peaceful; I decided to let you sleep."

Vince nodded at the book she clutched to her chest. "Well, what did you think now you've read the whole story?"

"I've read Tom's account on what happened way back then, which was chilling enough, but to read your dramatized account that fills in the gaps really brought home the terror Tom and the crew must have experienced. I'm certain Tom would agree with me when I say you have done his story justice, as I knew you would. I may be a little biased, but I think it's the best thing you've written to date."

Vince let out a relieved sigh. "Thank you, Lizzy, it means a lot. My agent thinks the same and is expecting sales to be good. There's even talk of it being made into a movie. Thanks again for letting me write Tom's story."

"You're very welcome, and I'm pleased for you, but if you don't invite me to the movie premiere, I will be upset."

Vince smiled. "VIP seat, I promise."

"I'm feeling tired, so if you put the book beside the bed so I can read it through again when I wake, I'll get some sleep. All this damn chemo and pills I've been having is draining my already frail body. They reckon they've seen evidence of improvement inside me, but I think they're just trying to give me hope."

"Well, I hope it's true. They say hope and positivity is a good healer." Vince placed the book on the bedside table and glanced at the wall clock. "I had better get going anyway as I'm already late for a meeting with my agent and publisher to finalize the details of the book's publicity campaign. I'll pop in again tomorrow if that's okay?"

Elizabeth smiled weakly. "If I'm still here, I'd welcome the company."

Unsure how to respond, Vince asked, "Do you want me to send a nurse in on my way out?"

Elizabeth raised a dismissive arm weakly and closed her eyes. "No, I'm sure they've got more important work to do than fuss over me."

"Okay, Lizzy, I'll see you tomorrow." He headed for the door, and as he went to close it, he saw that the frail woman had already drifted off to sleep.

Vince exited the room and gently closed the door.

At the end of the corridor, an alarm halted him. Fearing the worst, Vince turned to see nurses rushing to a room with a red light flashing beside the door. Relieved to see it wasn't Lizzy's room, he headed for the elevator.

EPILOGUE

Due to the extensive advertising campaign revolving around Tom's manuscript coming to light and the report issued by the Museum of Natural History experts presenting the arm as genuine and being from a new species they believed stretched back to prehistoric times, *Hell Ship* quickly rose up the book bestseller charts and reignited Vince's popularity. He appeared on chat shows both in the UK and America, where he talked about some of the events Tom had witnessed aboard the Fortuyn and his research into the Flying Dutchman myth.

To show viewers the creature in its entirety, Vince had a foot-high model of it created using Tom's sketch and descriptions, the arm, and advice from experts. Everyone who saw it was surprised at its formidable appearance. The creature model and Tom's descriptions of the larger monster were then used as a blueprint to design the creatures for the *Hell Ship* movie due out later that year.

Sitting in the front row of the London movie theater where the UK premiere of *Hell Ship* was about to be screened, Travis Atherton glanced behind at the actors, actresses, and some of the technical professionals responsible for bringing *Hell Ship* to the big screen, as well as the invited VIP guests which included some A-list celebrities. He then glanced at his watch again. "We can't wait any longer."

Vince glanced at the empty chair beside him. "Just five more minutes."

Travis sighed. "That's what you said ten minutes ago. If she were coming, she'd be here by now. I'm worried people will start leaving if the movie doesn't start soon, and we're on a time schedule. You and the stars have interviews set up afterward."

Reluctantly, Vince nodded. "Okay. Let them know they can start."

As Travis turned to raise his hand as a signal to the theatre manager waiting by the door to start screening the film, the door opened, and someone entered. He nudged Vince. "Your special VIP guest has finally arrived."

Vince climbed from his seat and hurried along the aisle towards the waiting woman. "Lizzy, you made it."

"Of course. I think battling cancer was less of an ordeal than negotiating London traffic."

Smiling, Vince crooked his arm. "I'll escort you to your seat."

Lizzy slipped her arm through his, and they walked down the aisle. Already informed of the reason for the delay and Lizzy's battle with cancer that she seemed to be winning, as well as her role in bringing Tom's manuscript to Vince, the audience rose to their feet and started clapping.

Surprised by the attention, Lizzy nudged Vince. "I feel like a celebrity."

"And so you should. None of us would be here if it weren't for you."

"Or Tom," Lizzy added.

"Or Tom," Vince confirmed.

When Lizzy sat in her seat, the clapping faded, the lights dimmed, and the curtains covering the screen swished open. All eyes focused on the screen when the movie began to play.

Lizzy smiled when the dedication to Tom and her appeared on the screen.

Hardly able to believe he was about to watch a movie adaptation of one of his books, a dream come true, Vince settled into the comfortable seat and watched the camera pan around the bookshop empty of customers and past the scowling bookshop owner. It stopped on the actor playing him who sat fiddling with his pen at a table stacked with unsold books.

Hell Ship Notes

Strange seaweed and creatures

The idea of using the seaweed and smaller crablike creatures in this story came from a small entry in a document discovered by a Dutchman I was put in touch with during my visit to Amsterdam. He had been collecting strange sea stories for a book he planned to write. Though he told me many weird and wonderful tales, one that stuck in my mind was the report he found in the Dutch East India archives concerning one of their vessels coming across a sinking ship. It is brief, as if the writer, who is thought to be a captain of a Dutch East India vessel making a report to his superiors about the wreck, was reluctant to say too much in fear of damaging his reputation.

This is the translated report:

Three days sailing from Cape Town, at day's end of March 18th 1724, calm sea, lowering sun highlighted wreckage of a sinking vessel to port. Four seamen rallied landing boat for closer inspection and discover vessel's name. On their return they report unknown Dutch East India ship was in bad repair. Sails ripped. Loose lines, broken stern mast, and was surrounded by seaweed with leaves the size of a man's torso and upward stalks. Strange sea creatures moved across it, which men called octopus crab, had long front limbs. No sign of crew or corpses spotted in water or aboard. Ship sunk dragging seaweed down with it. God rest their souls.

Though there is no evidence that it was the Fortuyn or any other ship that became the ghost ship The Flying Dutchman, the Fortuyn is as good a choice as any from the many that were lost without trace in the seas around the African coast.

Slave Trade

During the era of the barbaric transportation of slaves, the number of Africans who were transported the New World between 1520 and 1867 is estimated at 10 t0 15 million with an additional 4 to 6 million perishing en route.

<u>Images showing packing of Africans in Slave Ships</u>

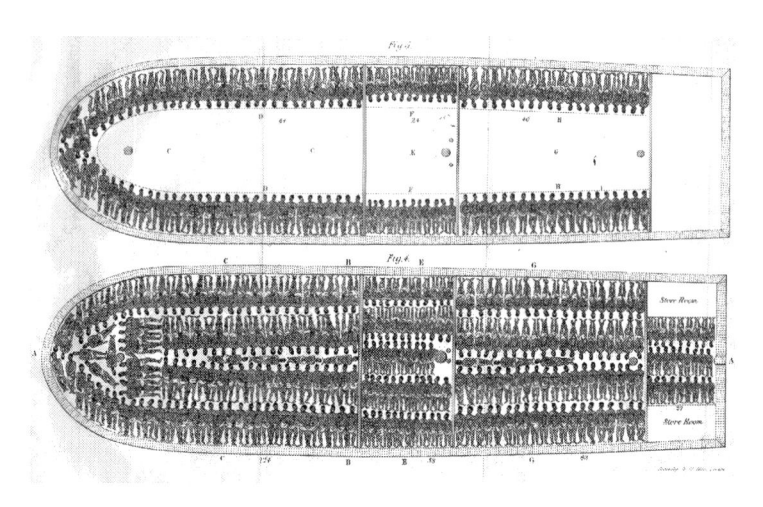

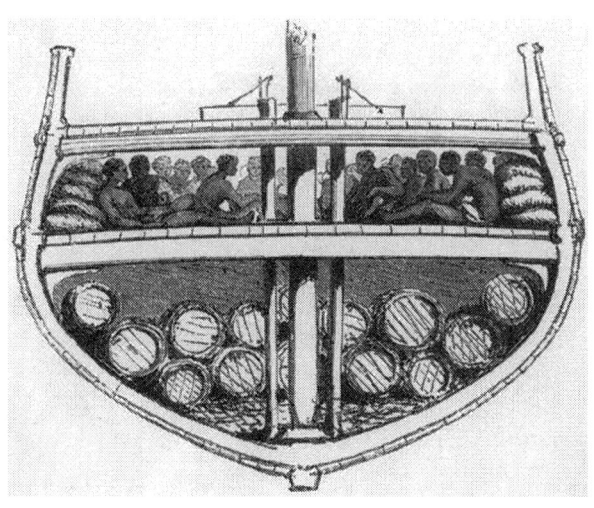

Note from Author

Thank you for purchasing and reading my book. I hope you found it an enjoyable experience. If so, could you please spread the word and perhaps consider posting a review on your place of purchase, it is the single most powerful thing you can do for me. It raises my visibility and many more people will learn about my book.

If you would like to be added to my mailing list to receive notifications of my new books, receive limited free advance review copies, occasional free books, send feedback or just to drop me a line, please contact me at: benhammott@gmail.com

Also by Ben Hammott

Horror Island

Where Nightmares Become Reality

-

Sarcophagus

Their mistake wasn't finding it, it was bringing it back!

--

ICE RIFT

ICE RIFT - SALVAGE

ICE RIFT - SIBERIA

The Lost City Book Series

EL DORADO Book 1: Search for the Lost City - An Unexpected Adventure

EL DORADO - Book 2: Fabled Lost Treasure - The Secret City'

--

Solomon's Treasure Series

BEGINNINGS: A Hunt for Treasure

THE PRIEST'S SECRET

(The Tomb, the Temple, the Treasure Book 1 and 2)

An ancient mystery, a lost treasure and the search for the most sought after relics in all antiquity.

A full list of Ben Hammott's books can be found on his author website:

www.benhammottbooks.com

44639558R00113

Printed in Poland
by Amazon Fulfillment
Poland Sp. z o.o., Wrocław